THE PADUAN CONSPIRACY

Roy Lewis

Published in 2012 by New Generation Publishing

First Edition

www.newgeneration-publishing.com

 New Generation Publishing

The discovery of a dead man at Chesters Fort meant that CI Cardinal's plans to smash the gang of his old adversary Clifford were thwarted. He assigns DS Grout to investigate the murder while he co-ordinates the hunt for gang-leader Clifford.

The investigation begins at Hadrian's Wall, leads to an University Archaeological department and a dealer in erotica in York, but a second murder—of a beautiful photographic model—sends Cardinal and Grout to the centre of an international art-smuggling organisation on the Bodensee.

There Grout faces death at the hands of a professional killer, before the trail seems to end, inconclusively, with a third murder in Amsterdam. The Clifford gang is broken but the identity of the killer can be discovered only when a separate matter is resolved—the riddle of the Paduan Conspiracy.

For further Roy Lewis crime titles visit www.roylewisbooks.com

PROLOGUE

They had sometimes called him Il Moro, because of his swarthy complexion, but that had been when he was a child.

It was many years now since he had heard the sobriquet: few dared use the sneering term once he had become the powerful and respected Lodovico Sforza, Duke of Milan.

Powerful, respected and ruthless. Naturally, his enemies—and there were many of them—might still call him Il Moro behind his back but they knew his reputation: they hated him for his ambitions, for his intrigues first with the French king, and when that monarch had shown his own greed for power in Milan, his alliance with Maximilian I, the Holy Roman Emperor. And there were some who whispered that it was Lodovico himself who was behind the mysterious death of his own nephew, a death that had opened the road to the dukedom for himself.

But there was another side to his personality: he was widely-read, an accomplished linguist, patron of the arts and, urged by the promptings of his young wife Beatrice, the man who had commissioned the magnificent painting The Last Supper, and who still acted as patron to the accomplished and almost legendary Leonardo da Vinci, the man who had orchestrated his wedding celebrations some years ago...

But Beatrice was sadly no more.

Lodovico stared blankly at the pages in front of him: he had been working on them for some hours and he was tired. He frowned as the image of Beatrice came to his mind. He had loved her well, but he was a virile man and there had of course been mistresses—Cecilia, who had borne him a son, Lucrezia on whom he had fathered two children. Beatrice had understood: he was a virile, lusty man. And now, as he wrestled with the political thoughts that danced in his head, the need to return in triumph to Milan, the machinations required to bind closely to him the princes who would support him in his bid to throw out the hated French from his dukedom, his loins stirred, not only at the memory of Beatrice but also at the thought that the time of his romantic assignation this night was now close.

Impatiently, he thrust aside the pile of papers and rose to his feet. Carlotta Fantini. He had seen her only once, when she had been pointed out to him in the Hall of Princes. She was reckoned to be a princess among courtesans and the glance she had bestowed upon him had told him that if he wished, she would be available.

He had made arrangements that very day.

He frowned. He was a man of precise habits. A few moments ago, somewhere in the city a bell had sounded the hour. It meant that Carlotta should be here by now. He had cast aside his work for the evening, dismissed his courtiers and awaited the woman. But it seemed she was late. The realisation angered him: he was the Duke of Milan. She was a mere courtesan, lovely and desirable though she might be. He would make her pay for her—

He caught the sound of a muffled cry from the anteroom to his apartment. He hesitated, then with mounting anger he strode towards the door. She had arrived, but some fool of a courtier must be preventing her entrance. He was impatient: the idiot who was intervening in the pursuit of the duke's pleasures would be made to feel the whip. His right hand instinctively grasped the hilt of the poniard that he wore at his belt as thoughts of violence intruded upon his lust.

He threw open the door.

The sight that greeted him riveted him to the spot for a moment. The room was shadowy but he could make out the forms of five men. And a woman. Carlotta.

Two of the strangers in the anteroom were holding her by the arms as she struggled frantically; a third had clasped his hands about her mouth to stifle her anguished cries. He saw briefly that her dress was torn, her breast exposed, and there was a dark stain at her waist. The other two men were momentarily confused by the duke's sudden appearance in the doorway and stood stock-still for a long moment, but then recovering, they were now rushing towards him.

Both men were armed and he saw the glitter of blades as they came for him.

The Duke of Milan was no coward and he had many times distinguished himself in battles. Moreover, he was a man of headstrong capabilities and the sight of the men rushing at him, and that of the woman struggling for her freedom and, perhaps, his life, brought a black rage upon him.

He roared a curse and flung himself upon his assailants drawing forth his poniard as he did so. They were astonished: they had probably expected that he would try to flee back into his chambers and his sudden attack caught them at a disadvantage. His blade flickered in the dim light as he slashed the throat of the nearest man in one swift movement and as the mortally injured assassin staggered sideways into his companion, knocking him off balance, the duke was thrusting at his second victim.

His blood was up, he was shouting loudly and he knew that in a matter of moments the alarm would be raised and his personal guards would storm into the room. But he himself would not await their arrival: in a blood rage he advanced upon the three men struggling with the half-fainting courtesan.

7

Sforza did not know how they would have gained entrance to his apartments. There would have been bribery involved and in due course he would find out who had betrayed him and the culprits would pay with their lives. He doubted that Carlotta herself would have been involved for she was injured and still struggling but as he dashed forward he realised that the swift turn of events had already caught the assassins off balance. The man trying to silence the courtesan had already released her, and was moving away out of range of the duke's fury; the other two men were seeking their blades, releasing Carlotta to face the raging duke. There was a hammering at the door, and moments later it burst open, the guards were rushing in and the three assassins sought escape.

The skirmish was brief. Sword blades glittered in the pale, flickering candlelight; two of the assailants had been cornered, the third had rushed past Sforza and dashed into the bedchamber, slamming the door shut behind him. The Duke of Milan raised Carlotta from the floor where she was half-swooning. Her wound was not serious, but the sight of her blood inflamed his passions even further.

He laid her down. The guards had cornered two of the assassins, and disarmed them. Sforza turned and raged back to his bedchamber, poniard in hand. The door held against him but he stormed at it with his shoulder: three blows and it gave way and he roared into the chamber, seeking the fifth assassin.

The room was empty. A curtain lifted in the night breeze. The window was open and as Sforza leaned out he could see the tiled roof stretching below him. He made out a dark figure frantically scrambling across the tiles, about to drop into the courtyard below.

Lodovico Sforza bellowed to his guards to hunt down the escaping man. He called for two of them to bring the unconscious Carlotta to his bed. He looked at her carefully as she lay there. She was indeed beautiful, and the wound was superficial. There would be another day...

He himself was unhurt. The attempted assassination had failed. The Duke of Milan had triumphed and heads would roll—after the rack and other implements had played their part on the bodies of the culprits who remained alive.

He took a deep breath, his anger receding as the adrenalin of triumph swept through his veins. Then, as he looked about him, some of that surge of triumph receded. He looked at the dressing table beside the bed. It had been swept clean.

One of the assassins had fled rather than fight, but he had not left empty-handed as he jumped from the window to the tiles.

The Duke of Milan clenched his fist. The two men apprehended by his guards would be racked, and feel the heat of the irons before they talked, and died.

As for the man who had escaped with the Duke's treasured possessions, there would be no part of Italy that he would be able to hide. The manhunt would begin this night.

CHAPTER ONE

Paul Gilbert completed the photographing of the statuary that interested him about five-o-clock in the afternoon. He spent the next half hour gathering up his equipment before taking one more look around the museum at Chesters Fort. He pondered over the commemorative stone that stated the pride felt by the men of the Tenth Legion at their completion of fifteen more paces of the Wall, and he thought again of the men who had travelled the length of the Roman Empire to work and fight on these northern hills. He inspected the Mithraic stone, symbol of the Roman Army's personal god, that had probably come from Brocolita, and considered returning to add some shots to his collection but finally decided against the idea. He had enough material from Chesters; tomorrow he'd move on to the site at Housesteads where a replica of the Roman fort had been erected and where considerable archaeological investigation was still continuing. He would also take the opportunity to walk a section of the Wall itself and look out over the hills where the barbarians had threatened the northern limits of the ancient empire.

Outside it was warm. The breeze had dropped and as he walked past the remains of the commandant's house, the low wall of the barracks and looked out across the slopes to the river he reflected how all this peace would be far divorced from the ancient reality of the blood, the howl of the icy northern winds, the screaming of dark savages as they attempted to storm the milecastles that held them back from the rich lands to the south. He would write about such thoughts in his next book of photographic essays.

Gilbert packed his equipment into the boot of his four wheel drive—useful for investigating along the muddy tracks in the Cumbrian hills—and drove on down to the George Hotel at Chollerford. He carefully unpacked all his gear and carried it all up to his room: he was a cautious man and the equipment had cost him a great deal of money.

After a shower he felt refreshed: he looked at himself in the mirror as he towelled himself down. He was still slim at forty: his fair hair was thinning a little at the crown but he was still presentable, he considered: clear eyes, good profile, only a hint of sagging at his jowls. He wandered out of the bathroom to the window and looked out over the terrace and the river bridge.

That was when he saw her.

She was standing in the gardens, quite alone, staring out towards the river bridge. She was tall, slimly built, long- legged, and she stood there with a casual, unaffected grace. Her skin was tanned, her hair black, cut short to the graceful line of her neck. The thin red sweater she wore exposed her upper arms and was low cut to the swell of her bosom. He could not make out her features since she was half turned away from him and she wore dark glasses, but he had no doubt that she was a beautiful woman.

Paul stood watching her for several minutes as his body dried under the towel he had draped around his waist, Unaware of his attention she stretched her arms, looked up at the late afternoon sky, then strolled along the path out of his line of sight.

He sighed. After she had disappeared he regretted he had not had the presence of mind to reach for his camera, getting a shot not so much for his book but merely for his own pleasure. There had been something about her that had stirred him. He had not been in a relationship for some time now, travelling about the north as he had been, and the woman had a grace about her that reminded him of a panther, wild, free, untamed.

He chewed at his lip, slightly annoyed with himself and then almost on cue she came back into his view. She had removed her dark glasses. Paul turned away, grabbed up his camera, clipped on the telephoto lens and waited until she paced a little nearer to his window.

He took several shots; they would be good since almost unconsciously she seemed to move about almost taking classical poses. He wondered what she would look like undressed.

She finally moved back towards the hotel, out of sight. He felt a vague excitement in his chest. He would be having dinner at the hotel. There was the chance she might be there...possibly alone. Paul Gilbert dressed carefully, with a barely subdued feeling of expectation. He had the premonition that the remainder of his stay at Chollerford was going to be interesting.

He experienced a feeling of acute disappointment when she failed to appear in the dining room. The room was crowded: a large number of people would seem to have come out from Newcastle for some kind of celebration and Gilbert was forced to relinquish the table he preferred, located near the window with a view over the gardens. His was a single table, near the door. It gave him a view of the whole room, but the woman he was looking for did not appear.

He was not disappointed later in the evening. He went to the bar and sat quietly, a little morose in the corner; while he sipped his drink he observed the room but there was no one there who aroused his interest. He was still there when the bar gradually emptied and the group of diners—a cricket club it would seem—disappeared back to Newcastle. Eleven-o-clock was chiming when the girl came in.

She looked at him; her glance held his for a few seconds. She had bright, sharp blue eyes, but there was something promisingly languorous in her eyes..

She moved towards the bar where the barman, who had earlier showed signs of hoping that his solitary customer would give up and go to bed, welcomed her with an ingratiating smile. Gilbert heard her ask for a whisky straight. She eyed the clock and then suggested that the barman might wish to serve her in the residents lounge. He nodded, she left, glancing briefly at Gilbert as she did so and after a moment the photographer rose and followed her into the lounge.

A man had to take his chances when they arose.

She was seated, one leg crossed elegantly over the other on a settee near the window. Outside the evening was darkening, the deep blue of northern summer evenings with a last fading glow of the dying sun. He stood over her, smiling, with his half empty glass in his hand.

'Bit late to start drinking,' he suggested.

She looked at him coolly, but made no reply. As he stood there, feeling slightly foolish, the barman came in with a tray and the whisky. Gilbert took the bill from the tray as he gave the drink to the girl and quickly signed it. The girl stared at him with cool eyes but raised no objection to his action.

After the barman had gone he said, 'Didn't see you at dinner.'

She shrugged.

She seemed distant yet she had accepted his paying for her drink, and there was something in her languorous attitude that made him feel his time would not be wasted.

'So,' he said slowly. 'I'm interested. Are you?'

He could read nothing in her eyes. 'In what?' she asked after a few moments.

'In carrying on this conversation for a few hours.'

'I didn't think we were having a conversation.'

'It could develop into one. Or something else.'

There was a hint of a smile upon her lips. They had a luscious curve to them. He felt he was making progress. He stared at her, grinning like an excited schoolboy. It seemed to him she was making up her mind about something, in a somewhat calculating fashion.

She showed her teeth in a smile: her teeth were white, even, and her smile seemed almost predatory. 'All right. I'm bored. I've nothing better to do, so, let's converse.'

'My name's Gilbert...Paul Gilbert. I'm an author of sorts...I produce photographic essays, really, and I'm doing one on Hadrian's Wall.'

'I would have thought that's a bit old hat...surely it's been done often before.'

He put her right on that score. Enthusiastically, he told her of the crags above WhinSill, the hills the centurions had watched, the savage raids of the men from the north; he tried to instil in her the excitement he felt at the exaltation of the height and history of the Wall but he realised after a little while he had not managed to overcome her bored air. He was a little disappointed and more than a little desperate: he had hoped she would have possessed intellectual qualities as well as beauty. Although he would settle for the latter, if truth be known. He suggested a walk on the terrace in the moonlight.

The moon was bright. It gleamed silver on the river. As they strolled, each with glass in hand, the girl's shoulder touched his briefly and he shivered. 'You haven't told me your name.'

She hesitated.

'Eileen.' She said at last and turned her face to his.

15

It was casual and yet meaningful. She raised her head slightly. It was with a certain surprise, mingled with excitement, that he kissed her. There was still a lingering disappointment in him when it was over: here kiss had been very practised, almost professional but he felt it was as though she was merely experimenting, trying to determine whether she really wanted to be kissed. It was a curious experience, but he was not the man to look a gift horse in the mouth, so to speak.

'How long are you staying at the George?'

'Just tonight.'

'Then we don't have much time, do we?'

'No. And it's beginning to get cold out here.'

This could be the start of something, he thought...or the end. He hoped it was the former. Certainly, there was something in her tone that suggested he should try his luck. So he asked, and she agreed almost immediately that they could share a d rink from her min-bar, but that she'd like to go ahead.

He stood on the terrace after she had gone, alone in the gathering darkness, as he finished his drink.

It was all happening so quickly, and yet there was something cold and calculated about it. Oddly enough that only served to increase his desire. His throat was dry. He had the impression she hardly saw him as a person, merely a man. He could have been anyone. A one night stand. Not that there was anything wrong with that. And though he liked directness he still felt in sexual matters there should be more...more of a civilized approach, a bantering, sexual innuendo, physical awareness, a savouring of the sexual opportunity. Like sipping good wine.

This had been too quick to be entirely satisfactory. But perhaps he was too much of a romantic. If she was available, why should he worry?

16

The thought of the girl's body excited him. Ten minutes, she had suggested, but what was a matter of a few minutes between friends? He left the terrace, walked through the lounge and took the stairs.

The corridor was quiet. She had told him she was in Room 14. When he reached her room he tapped lightly on the door with the tips of his fingers.

'Eileen?'

There was no reply.

He waited, tapped again, more heavily this time but there was still no reply. The exulting smile began to harden on his mouth, and he chewed his lower lip. He knocked again but the silence grew around him as an angry knot began to form in his stomach. A few minutes ago he had been feeling rather superior, feeling a vague disappointment that the girl hadn't played a long waiting game with him but now that feeling had evaporated: the ache in his loins was now a compound of desire and frustration and anger. He rapped his knuckles once more on the unresponsive door and then, as the fury began to mount in his chest he turned away, marched down the corridor, went back to his own room.

He walked the length of the room, time and again, clenching his fists in the darkness. His skin felt sharply sensitive, his mouth was dry, and there was a pounding anger in his head. The flash of a car's headlights briefly illuminated the darkness of his room and he caught a glimpse of himself in the mirror. His eyes were bright with anger.

He undressed quickly, throwing his clothing savagely to the floor. He lay on his back in the bed, staring sleeplessly at the ceiling.

His mood of black frustration lasted through till dawn, outliving the frenzied twisting sleep that he tossed through. When he went to the window he realised there had been a light rain during the night but the clouds had washed away under the morning sun and Gilbert showered at six, dressed, walked out of the hotel and made his way along the road eastwards towards Chesters.

He did not want to face the girl's cool triumph at breakfast: she had led him on, played with him, made a fool of him and he would not allow her the satisfaction of seeing his sour countenance. He took the footpath from Chollerford Bridge up to the abutment of the old Roman structure that had carried the walk and the Wall across the North Tyne. Lewis holes that had been used for lifting the great stone blocks of the bridge were visible still.

The phallus carved by a bored legionnaire centuries ago on one of the stones mocked him.

He walked briskly back down to Chesters Fort, the wind cool his burning face. He had an uninterrupted view of the river and all about him was quiet, the hills still under the morning sun. He cursed the girl. She had been playing with him; she had led him on and then she had lain in her bed, laughing into her pillow as he had knocked in frustration at her door. It would certainly not have been virginal fears that had made her bar the door to him: he remembered the confident expertise of her kiss.

He was unable to fathom why she had behaved the way she had, and the nagging ache was still in his body. He walked through the car park, paying little attention to the solitary car parked there. The gate to Chesters was open and he walked through, his hands in his pockets, shoulders hunched disconsolately.

The mood left him when he reached the ancient bath-house. He stood on the remains of the Roman walls and looked down to what had been the hot bath and the latrines and he walked over them to look at the Tyne where it curved in a long slow bend at the bottom of the slope.

It was then that he saw the man's fingers.

They were curling lifelessly, half closed. Against the rough hewn stone of the bath-house wall the dead thumb was cocked in a macabre gesture of male triumph.

CHAPTER TWO

It was not the screaming from the next door apartment that offended Chief Inspector James Cardinal.

After all, the noise was connected to perfectly legitimate sexual activity on the part of the neighbours and was therefore none of his business. But his wife saw it in a different light. It was, she advised him, like living next door to a brothel. He was not sure how she felt able to make this comparison, having led as far as he was aware a somewhat sheltered life. And secretly he rather envied the vigorous activity that seemed to be going on next door: his own marriage held no such excitements. What offended him was his wife's insistence that he should do something about it. She argued "What was the point in being a policeman if one couldn't sort such things out?" It was her constant complaint. It gave him a headache, one more fierce and less convenient than the one she regularly pleaded at weekends.

As a consequence, when he entered the office on Monday morning he was in a bad temper, his brow furrowed with pain, unwilling as usual to seek relief in painkilling drugs, deeming it more appropriate to fight the pain by normal, natural means. His mood was not improved by the sight of Detective Sergeant Grout seated in cardinal's chair in the office. Grout was a good man, a solid, dependable officer endowed with flashes of flair and intelligence, the sort of man Cardinal needed to supplement his own qualities of dogged persistence backed by hard work. But there were occasions when Cardinal regretted that he had invited Grout to join him in the regional Crime Squad at York. The fact was that Cardinal sometimes found Grout a bit too much to bear.

He hadn't tried to work out why. Physically they were very different: Cardinal was tall, lean, narrow-featured; Grout was of a stocky peasant build, broad-shouldered with a disarmingly open visage. There was the fact that Grout was reading Law in his spare time—which Cardinal tried to keep to a minimum—and had acquired a working knowledge of Urdu, of all things, while James Cardinal thought only of putting his feet up during the rare occasions when he found himself not occupied in or pondering over the cases he was currently working on. But added to all this was the fact that Grout was of a personality that seemed difficult to ruffle: when Cardinal snarled at him grout showed little reaction other than a setting of the lips and the raising of his chin a trifle.

This irritated Cardinal, and left him with a vague feeling of inferiority, even if he was the senior officer.

Grout scrambled out of the chair as Cardinal came in, scowled at him, and then stood in front of the window, massaging his temple with probing fingers. Grout was there because Cardinal had summoned him, but the chief inspector was in no hurry to explain the reason: it would do Grout good to be kept waiting.

'Did you finish the report on the Elstrom manslaughter charge?' Cardinal asked at last, staring sightlessly out of the window.

'It's on your desk, sir.'

'And the bribery offence?'

'It's with Maggie, being typed up. She reckons it'll be completed early this afternoon.'

Maggie. Cardinal flicked an angry glance over his shoulder. He did not approve of familiarity with the civilian staff. Grout seemed generally popular in headquarters and adapted socially with much more ease that Cardinal was capable of. He gritted his teeth, turned away from the window and sat in the chair behind his desk. Grout remained standing. Cardinal eyed him sourly. 'You've put in for leave.'

'That's right, sir.'

'You're aware your work with the Squad must come first.'

'Of course, sir.'

'Time off will be difficult to organise.'

Grout nodded. 'I'm aware of the work load.'

'Well, if I am to release you it will have to wait until we sort out this Clifford business.'

'Clifford?'

'Ah. I haven't told you about Clifford, Grout.' Cardinal bared his teeth in a thoughtful grimace. 'Clifford...it's a sort of long-standing thing, you might even say it's developed into a sort of personal vendetta as far as I'm concerned. If there's one man in the world I'd like to see slammed into a cell it's Clifford.'

'I've not heard of him, sir.'

'No.' Cardinal was silent for a little while, frowning. He wished this bloody headache would subside. Thought of Clifford only made it worse. He stared at his slim, elegant hands placed on the desk in front of him. The Clifford thing went back a long way, back to Cardinal's early days as an inspector, before the Regional Crime Squad had been formed, before Cardinal had come north.

In a sense it demonstrated Clifford's efficiency and cunning: while the man's evasiveness was partly due to the restrictions that hampered police work he was also a remarkable slippery customer. On three occasions Clifford had been hauled in on serious charges, only to escape scot-free when witnesses disappeared, or changed their testimony...and once on a legal technicality concerning which Cardinal had been hauled over the coals for letting dislike blind his

22

judgement. 'He's a very criminal character, is Clifford,' Cardinal acknowledged bitterly.

'He's here in the north, sir?'

Cardinal swivelled in his chair so he could see the map of northern England pinned to the wall. His domain, his manor, the area covered by the regional Crime Squad was delineated in red. He nodded towards the map. 'You see that, Grout? I wouldn't mind that Clifford's got one just like it in his office, wherever his bloody office is. He's no fool and he's a good organiser. He first came to my notice when I was with the Metropolitan Police: he was involved in the protection rackets in those days, before he moved into prostitution. By the time we finally managed to crack down on that business, with a certain success, he had moved on and he opened up other sidelines, like smuggling cigarettes on an industrial scale, though his main business soon became the distribution of drugs. We tried to put him inside for the establishment of bogus companies and fraud scams but he could afford a smart Queen's Counsel who made a fool of us and our efforts. We were left with egg on our faces, and he was there laughing at us.'

Cardinal glowered at the map, massaged his temples again, almost unconsciously as the pent-up anger in his chest began to get the better of him.

'Since then, he's moved into a new racket, I'm informed. You know much about the art world, Grout?'

'I know a Constable from a Sargent, sir.'

Cardinal turned his chair slowly around to glare at the detective sergeant. 'I can do without the laboured humour, Grout.' He grimaced, then sighed despondently. 'Clifford moved into the art world some years ago in style. We believe he organised most of the big art thefts in the London area over the last five years but apart from paintings he's also moved into a

23

lucrative system of scams involving antiques. There's a packet to be made from the States and Europe. A lot of the stuff is looted from designated—and protected—sites scattered throughout Europe and in particularly Italy and there are always unscrupulous museums, publicly endowed as well as private, prepared to accept the doubtful provenance that Clifford's associates are able to provide. Clifford has a network throughout Europe, and has been selling to the States, China, Switzerland—where's he's got a warehouse hidden away somewhere, but he's now carved up the whole country into organised area. He's got ten territories, each with a nominated agent at its head, responsible to him. There's the South West, the South, the Metropolitan, the south east to cover that part of the country. Farther north he's got a midland area organised from Birmingham, a north western based in Liverpool, a Yorkshire, northern and Scottish series of operations.'

'You said ten territories, sir.'

'We mustn't forget Wales, Grout,' Cardinal said dryly. 'If you spoke Welsh instead of bloody Urdu I'd be inclined to send you down there.'

Grout hesitated, ignoring the gibe.

'How exactly are you involved in all this, sir?'

'The fact of the matter,' Cardinal said, 'is that when I was with the Met I was the officer in charge when we finally pulled in Clifford. I got to know him well. We're hunting him down now after some new information came in: the other Regional Squads are involved but because of my knowledge of the bastard I'm to co-ordinate the hunt. I'm telling you all this, Grout, to explain why I won't be around much to assist you during the coming weeks.'

Grout frowned. 'Assist?'

'I do sometimes wonder who's running this bloody office,' Cardinal said.

Grout stiffened but made no response.

'Maggie,' Cardinal growled in contempt. When Grout showed no reaction, he went on. 'Anyway, I was down in London on Friday at a conference of the regional senior officers. It looks as though we've struck lucky at last. A certain disaffected gentleman has seen fit to rat on Clifford—faced as he is with a lengthy term inside for fraud—and we are told there is shortly to be a meeting of the Board'

'I don't understand, sir,' Grout murmured.

'Clifford has what he calls a Board...the heads of his areas, and they are to meet in London tomorrow. We are lined up to pounce on them. Not only will they all be conveniently there but there should be enough in their individual briefcases to put them all away for a lot of years. Even so, once we get them in the net there's going to be a lot of weeks to sort things out so it's unlikely you be getting Inspector rank until I get back. The paperwork, you know. And as for leave...well, you see how it is.'

Grout had not been aware he was in line for promotion. He opened his mouth in surprise but Cardinal cut him off coldly before he could speak. 'Don't let it get to your head, Grout.' He got up walked across to the map on the wall, prodded at it with his lean finger, traced the line along the Yorkshire border. 'Inspector Elliott will go down to London this afternoon and I'll be awaiting confirmation that the northern boss will have boarded the train. We've been tagging him for some time: he never flies down because of the documentation required. The rest of the mob will be converging for the meeting this afternoon and tonight. We know the location. We have the troops on standby. Tomorrow we'll catch them like rats in a trap.'

Cardinal suddenly became aware of the gloating tone in his voice. He returned abruptly to his desk and sat down once more. 'So, I called you in to tell you how it is: I won't be around much over the next few weeks. I'll be pretty busy with the Clifford business. That means you'll needs to pick up the overview on the Endbury and Cooper cases from Inspector Maxwell. He'll be taking over some of my duties, acting as my deputy, and — '

Cardinal was interrupted by a knock on the door. He raised his head and called out. The door opened and a fresh-faced young constable from the outer office entered the room.

'This had better be important,' Cardinal snarled.

The young constable licked his lips nervously, glanced at Grout. Cardinal could guess what the young man would be saying when he got back with his colleagues: His Eminence is in a right mood today.

'This message has just come in from Chief Superintendent Carliss, sir. I thought you'd want to see it immediately.' Cardinal took the proffered paper and read it quickly. His lean features took on a grimmer aspect. His lips writhed back as he gestured to the constable to leave and then As Grout waited patiently Cardinal picked up the phone and dialled a London number. He waited, tapping his fingers impatiently on the desk.

'Bill? Cardinal here. I've just got the message. What the hell's going on?'

Grout waited and watched as Cardinal's mouth drooped in ill-disguised disappointment. The chief inspector said nothing more during the next two minutes as the man at the other end of the phone continued. When Cardinal did finally speak, he was terse. 'That puts us back where we started. Right. I'll see what I can do this end to try to pull them in.'

He banged down the receiver in obvious anger. He glared at Grout, as though blaming him for what had happened. 'Bloody meeting's cancelled.'

'Clifford's meeting, you mean?'

'What other meeting would I be talking about?' Cardinal said savagely. 'The meeting's cancelled and as far as I can gather our informant, our inside man is reckoning that all the area heads have been ordered to go to ground. Wherever they can find a personal rat hole.'

Grout hesitated. 'So what happens now?'

'We'll have to scrabble around the regions to pull in the bastards one by one,' Cardinal said with an angry snap to his ton. 'And that means a lot of hard work and trouble. We'll not have all the evidence we need, in some cases all we can do is put a scare into them, alert them, maybe fix them with receiving if we can find their local warehouse, but the whole damn thing is a mess, Grout, believe me, a real mess.'

Cardinal rose abruptly, marched to the door, flung it open and bawled, 'Where the hell's Robinson? Why hasn't he reported in yet?'

Hastily, Grout pushed past the senior officer and stepped into the corridor. 'I'll check at once, sir, and get a call out to the patrol car.'

'Contact Inspector Parker at Leeds while you're at it. Fill him in, ask for his co-operation and he'll know what you mean when you say that Elliot needs to be brought in for questioning.'

As Grout made his way to the outer office Cardinal walked back into his room and banged the door behind him. He stood by the window, gradually cooling down, suppressing the painful ache of anger in his chest. The way things were going on he'd probably end up with a heart attack. Clifford, the neighbours, his wife's constant complaints...he stared out across the sunlit roofs to the ancient cathedral where the tourists would be thronging, through the Shambles, along the city walls, past Clifford's Tower. He wondered whether his old enemy might have been distantly related to the Norman robber baron who had built the tower: the follower of Duke William the Conqueror would no doubt have been as violent and unprincipled as the man who had been getting under Cardinal's skin for years.

Several minutes passed before the telephone on Cardinal's desk rang. He picked up the receiver. 'Robinson?'

Robinson's voice was partly masked by the sound of traffic roaring in the background. 'Yes, sir. Sorry I've not called in but I thought I'd better wait to see if our friend took the next train out of Newcastle.'

'He wasn't on the first?" Cardinal asked, glancing at his watch.

'No, sir. Anything gone wrong?'

'You could bloody well say so. The meeting's been cancelled. That's why you're looking out for Rigby is useless: he won't be heading south. He's off to the woods somewhere.'

'So what now?'

'Pick him up if you can. You've got some men on standby, and someone on surveillance at his home. Get there straight away. I'll send a couple of squad cars as backup but you'd better liaise as of right not with the Newcastle and Northumberland police at Ponteland, keep them in the picture. For God's sake let's have no slip-ups. I want you to bring Rigby here to me at York, alive and kicking, along with Elliot. Alive, kicking, and I hope squealing their ugly heads off!'

'I'll get things moving straight away, sir.'

Robinson rang off.

Cardinal replaced the receiver, stared at it for several seconds then looked up as Detective Sergeant

Grout tapped on the door and entered. Cardinal didn't like what he saw. The normally expressionless sergeant was frowning and his thick lips were set. Cardinal had rarely seen that expression. It meant inevitably there was a problem.

'Tell me,' Cardinal said wearily.

'You've spoken to Robinson?'

'I have. Rigby didn't turn up to take the train to London for the Board meeting.'

Grout nodded as though he already knew. He had a slip of paper in his hand, a message from the operations room.

'This came in earlier, sir. It wasn't drawn to our attention because the duty sergeant didn't realise its significance and thought Inspector Maxwell should be the man to deal with it but—'

'Spit it out, Grout!'

'Robinson won't have any difficulty finding Rigby, whom I gather is one of Clifford's associates.'

"How do you work that out?"

'Joseph Frederick Rigby was discovered early this morning at Chesters Fort in Northumberland. The back of his head was battered in. He's very dead, sir. As a doornail, one might say.'

Cardinal sighed. There was something quite old-fashioned about Detective Sergeant Grout.

CHAPTER THREE

Grout guessed that there would be a certain amount of pressure on the parking space at Chesters so he left his car at the George Hotel car park and walked the short distance past the bridge towards the ancient Roman camp. The narrow road that swung up the hill to his right was part of the old Roman military way that slice through the hard quartz dolerite hills towards Carlisle but Chesters Fort lay beyond the narrow belt of trees ahead of him.

The parking area beyond the first gate was guarded by two uniformed policemen and the entrance was taped off. Some disconsolate gentlemen of the Press were standing by, clearly niggled by the paucity of information that had been provided them. They stepped aside as Grout pushed his way past them, only one of them half-heartedly raising a hand and asking a question but Grout ignored him, presented his identity card to the officers, and was allowed to step inside the perimeter sealed off with tape.

He made his way towards the cluster of officers huddled near the entrance to Chesters Museum and introduced himself. The burly, chubby-featured inspector looked him up and down. 'Grout. Regional Crime Squad, hey?' The man's eyes had narrowed suspiciously, squinting against the brightness of the sun. 'So what's your interest in this business?'

'The dead man is called Rigby.'

'We know that.'

'We were going to pull him in today.'

'He won't be telling you much now.' The inspector writhed back his lips in a grimace. 'Not with a hole in the back of his head.'

Grout recognised the truculence in the man's tone: he was aware of it and had expected it. He had felt the same way himself, in Leeds, before he had joined the Regional Crime Squad. It was a matter of manors, of responsibilities, of turf wars. He waited, until the officer spoke again.

'I'm Inspector Waters. So what exactly do you want around here?'

Grout shrugged. His tone was neutral, careful. 'We'd like to know the circumstances surrounding the man's death. He was due to be pulled in for questioning with regard to a national enquiry that's been under way. It may be there's something significant our own investigations will turn up. Apart from what you find, I mean. We'd appreciate your co-operation.'

'And you'll get it,' Inspector Waters murmured with a lack of conviction in his tone. He paused, reflecting. 'He's known to us, of course. Petty villainy, bit of a record, and he'll be no loss to the community. Our guess is he's been clobbered in some gang quarrel or other...We better get something straight though, Grout. You got no standing here, right?'

'I'm aware of that, Inspector.'

Waters was little mollified by the quick assurance offered. 'This will be a locally controlled investigation...until I hear otherwise from the Chief Constable at Ponteland. I'm not interested in what the Regional Crime Squad have got on Rigby unless it can bring a quick end to our own enquiries. So, I've no objection to your keeping a watching brief on all this, provided you don't get in my way, but I want you to be clear about this: I won't accept interference. This is my operation. Beyond that,' he waved his hand in a magnanimous gesture, 'help yourself. Don't get too close to the crime scene, of course: forensic haven't finished yet. Like, don't get in the way. Otherwise...'

He was about to turn away when Grout asked, 'Where was the body found?'

'Down there, near the bath-house. Here...' He called to a young constable standing nearby. 'Stocks, this is DS Grout. Stocks will show you the location, answer any questions you got, and keep you out of mischief. That right, Stocks? OK. But before you leave the site, DS Grout, perhaps you'll have another word with me. So you can sort of fill me in about the Regional Crime Squad interest. That sort of thing. I'll probably be inside the museum.'

Constable Stocks nodded affably to Grout and led the way towards the low walls of the bath-house, excavated many years ago. They tramped across the sward avoiding the churned ruts that had baked hard in the sun and wind, skirted the remains of what had been the Roman commandant's house and crossed the trimmed grass where a screen had been erected. It covered the lower part of the Roman structure that had served as a bath-house and latrines: under cover Grout saw three white-coated technicians at work, with a sports-jacketed civilian overseeing the work. Grout guessed he'd be the forensic scientist brought in from the laboratory at Gosforth.

'I think they'll be carting the body off pretty soon,' Stocks murmured. 'Looks like they've all but finished. Senior pathologist, he's been and gone already. They're just tidying up now, I think.' There was a certain self-importance in the constable's tone, an attempt to leave the impression that this was all in a day's work for him. Grout doubted that. It was likely this was Stocks's first murder case. But he would never admit that to an outsider.

The plastic shell was waiting its burden. Grout stepped into the tent. The body had now been moved but that didn't concern him much: the photographers would have done their job. But he was curious to get a glimpse of the man called Rigby: the features were fixed and waxen now but Grout guessed the dead man would have been in his mid-thirties when his life was brought to an abrupt and violent end. About five feet nine, he calculated, hair thinning in the front, cheekbones that now seemed to jut through skin that had become almost transparent in death.

'Back of his head was crushed in,' Constable Stocks said conversationally. 'Wouldn't be surprised that he had it coming to him. Like Inspector Waters said, he's known to us. I believe he's got a record, but nothing of recent years. Started with twocking cars down in the West End. Bit of drug dealing in South Shields too, I believe. But not recently. Been quiet, like. Moved into other stuff I guess. Bigger deals, with the East European girl trade and that sort of thing. That's the chat. Romanian whores. I always think they're handsome women those Romanians. Anyway...'

'Anything of significance found on the body?' Grout interrupted.

'Dunno about that, I just been up here an hour or so, but Inspector Waters will be able to fill you in on all that sort of thing. But from what I can make out it looks as though he wasn't actually killed here. He got his head bashed in somewhere up near the museum. He was dragged down here afterwards. To hide the body I suppose, chance to gain a few hours, I expect.'

'So who found him?'

Constable Stocks screwed up his eyes, wrinkled his nose. 'Ah, it was some guy called Gilbert, I believe. He was out for a stroll in the early morning. They been questioning him down at the George this morning. Think he's been taken into Newcastle by now.'

'Have forensics come up with a likely time of death?'

'Like always,' the young constable announced importantly, 'they wouldn't say straight off but the lads tell me they did give a rough sort of estimate. They think it was about midnight or maybe early hours of this morning.'

'But he was killed up there, near the museum,' Grout murmured, looking back to the entrance where he had briefly met Inspector Waters.

'Yeah, that's right. You won't know, of course, but the museum got broken into last night. Could have been Rigby, but it could have been the man who clobbered him, as well.'

'So was anything taken from the museum' Grout asked.

'Can't say. They're still checking that I think. Inspector Waters, he'll be the one to ask about that.' The constable had reddened somewhat; perhaps he suddenly felt he had been talking too much to an officer he did not know, and one from outside the force.

'Yeah. Maybe I'd better do that. Thanks anyway'

Grout took another walk around the bath-house as a matter of interest, historical rather than police procedural for he knew full well he would find nothing the locals or the forensic team would have missed. Then he made his way back across the field towards the museum building.

The uniformed policeman at the entrance looked bored, standing to one side of the door in the shade. He told Grout that the inspector was to be found in the storeroom so Grout entered the building and wandered through the rooms, glancing at some of the exhibits, seeing nothing exceptionally interesting. He knew there was a more extensive museum now located at Housesteads, complete with facsimile copies of the letters written by the wife of the Roman commandant two thousand years ago, inviting friends to dinner, listing items to be bought for meals, trivia that were fascinating to the modern mind, showing that nothing really had changed in society over the centuries. He moved towards the steps leading down to the storeroom

Inspector Waters was standing at the foot of the steps, just inside the door, talking to the curator. He glanced up, saw Grout, then ignored his presence. There was dust in the air; the smell of inadequate ventilation touched Grout's nostrils.

Grout stood in the doorway, looking over the inspector's shoulder. Upstairs the exhibits had been carefully arranged, ticketed, described, but down here the items stored had been placed on shelves without description. He noted a few pieces of statuary in poor condition and it was clear that English Heritage had clearly placed most figurines of interest upstairs, or had moved them to the more tourist-orientated museum at Housesteads, some miles away, where excavations were still continuing and the replica milecastle had been built.

Grout was aware that over the centuries much of the stone of Hadrian's Wall had suffered from the depredations of farmers and sheepherders who had used Roman-cut stone to build their walls and shelters over the years.

Inspector Waters turned to glance at Grout.

'Had a look around then?'

'Yes, thank you,' Grout replied quietly. 'Constable Stocks was most helpful. But I understand there was a break-in here as well...as well as the killing up above.'

The curator muttered indignantly. He was an elderly, small man with a narrow, wind-lined face. Grout guessed he would have been working here for many years, and this was the first time events of such a catastrophic nature would have occurred on his watch. He was clearly as upset by the desecration of his kingdom as by the fact of a death at the site.

'Disgraceful,' he muttered. 'Quite disgraceful.'

'Has anything of value been taken?' Grout asked as Inspector Waters, cold-eyed, stood aside.

'Everything here is of value,' the curator snapped.

'Yes, but—'

'Can't understand,' the police inspector intervened, 'can't understand why anyone would want to break in here. Value, you say? In my view there's nothing of real value except to students of history and tourists. Anyway, as far as we can see nothing's been taken anyway. Is that not right?' he challenged the curator.

'That's not the point!' the curator snapped. 'The fact there's been a break-in, that's enough! Anyway, I haven't really had time to make an absolutely detailed check but it doesn't look as though any of the exhibits up above have been touched.'

'What about down here?' Grout asked.

The little man shook his head, rubbed a doubtful finger against his nose and looked back behind him. 'There's been some disturbance here, but nothing seems to be missing. You must realise all items of real significance are kept up above. Down here we have items that are still open to study, or which can be used by students from university archaeological departments as examples...like that Mithraic stone over there. I remember the day when they found the Mithraic temple on the Wall. Before that everyone thought he was just a minor deity of Persian origin, but once the temple was unearthed it soon became clear that Mithras was a powerful god, the favourite deity of the Roman army, a god who—'

'Yes, yes,' Waters intervened brusquely. It was clear to Grout that the inspector had already been subjected to a barrage of unwanted historical information by the little curator. 'That'll do for now, at any rate. You need to carry out a thorough check both upstairs and down here to ensure that nothing really has been taken. The sooner you can let us have a definitive statement, the better. It may well be the break-in is linked to the murder, but on the other hand it might have been someone other than the killer, or Rigby himself, who was messing around about here. In which case, who knows? Maybe we have a witness to what went on up above.' He grimaced at the curator and patted his shoulder. 'Anything you can come up with, it could be important.'

The curator led the way back up the stairs after closing the storeroom door. It was unlocked, Grout noted. At the top of the stairs Inspector Waters watched the curator amble off to his office, presumably to retrieve the books in which records of the holdings would be kept and then he sighed, gazed around him. The tiny dust motes drifted about them, dancing and flickering in the sunlight that came in through the high window. Waters shook his head. 'Beats me why anyone would want to break in here and lump out any of this lot. Could have been kids, of course, just out to vandalise the place. Maybe disturbed by what went on with Rigby, they scarpered back to wherever they came from. Chances of finding them are remote, is my guess. Young layabouts from the West End...'

'Long way to come to break in here,' Grout pondered. 'What would they be after?'

'Entrance money? I got no idea. Who knows what goes through the heads of kids these days?'

'It could have been Rigby who broke in.'

Inspector Waters stared at Grout for a few moments. 'Maybe. The forensic boys may come up with something to support that idea. But what the hell would a villain like Rigby expect to find in this God-forsaken place?'

Carefully, Grout suggested, 'He's been involved in some dicey dealings involving works of art.'

Waters stared at him. 'I see. That's why the Crime Squad is interested in Rigby, hey? Art thefts. But there's no bloody Picassos or da Vincis here, believe me. Nothing I can see here which would be tempting to an art thief. Still...you had a look around. Did your own perfectly trained eye,' he added sarcastically, 'pick up anything us local yokels might have missed?'

Grout shook his head. 'I just wanted to check out the location. I'm sure your team will have done all that's necessary.'

'Pleased to have your approbation,' Waters grunted unenthusiastically. 'Anyway, I'm through here for the time being. I'm off back down to the George. We been taking statements from some of the staff down there so I'd better see how things are going.'

'Is it OK if I come along?' Grout asked.

The inspector hesitated, grimaced. 'I'm not sure it'll do you any good. You'll have access to our report, I guess, in due course. Once it's been cleared back in Ponteland. Thing is, you'll just be under our feet, you know what I mean. But I'll check it out. Now I need to get on.'

Grout was not surprised by the man's attitude. There was always local resistance to outside interference. Or even assistance. As Inspector Waters ambled out of the museum to make his way back to his car Grout wandered in the direction taken by the curator. He found him seated in his office, poring over some heavy ledgers and a catalogue. He glanced up at Grout, then chose to ignore his presence. He rose, clutching the catalogue and went back to the exhibit room, checking off the items, clucking his tongue quietly as he did so. Grout watched him for a while. He could understand the doubts in Inspector Waters's mind: there could hardly be anything here that would attract a thief of Rigby's inclination...or even young thugs from the west

End for that matter. But what was Rigby doing out here at Chesters anyway?

'You have all this material catalogued,' Grout said, 'but what of the stuff in the storeroom below? Do you have a list of all the items there?'

The curator jerked his narrow head in surprise as though he had forgotten Grout's presence. He frowned. 'No catalogue, no. It's unimportant stuff. On the other hand the University Archaeological department uses stuff down there as a teaching resource, have borrowed items from time to time, arrange visits here for some of the students as well as encourage them to do work on the dig still going on up at Housesteads. So they'll have a pretty good idea of what's down there, especially since professor Godfrey has been in charge of their Antiquities section. He's made extensive use of our facilities of recent years.'

'Professor Godfrey?'

'Yes, you must have heard of him. Quite an authority on Roman antiquities, oh, yes, indeed. He wrote a monograph on the Wall a few years back...we have a copy up in the exhibition, in fact, most instructive, most instructive. The wall and the milecastles and Mithraic influences...He's encouraged his students to use our facilities a great deal. It was his section that sponsored the survey that was done here last year...but no, sorry, there's no catalogue as such regarding the materials here. But I'm sure Professor Godfrey can assist you.'

Grout could tell the curator was a little embarrassed that there seemed to be a flaw in the security procedures used at the museum. There seemed little point in flustering him further. He nodded, and walked away, back into the sunlight.

He was surprised to see that Inspector Waters was still there, getting out of his car. The officer waved his mobile at Grout. 'Just been in touch with HQ. Had a call. It seems your chap—Cardinal, is it? He's cleared lines with the Chief Constable. We are supposed to offer you freedom of the manor, so to speak. You can come along to the George while we're taking statements.' He stared at Grout, making little attempt to hide the animosity in his eyes. 'But let's be clear about one thing. Whatever your boss, and for that matter the Chief Constable says, you still got no standing in this business. We run the operational unit, this is our scene of crime, and while you can listen in, I don't want you under our feet. Capisce?'

It was probably the only Italian Inspector Waters knew. It would have been gleaned from films such as The Godfather.

Grout nodded. He smiled slightly as the inspector turned back to his car. Even the engine roaring into life seemed to throw out a measure of defiance to the powers that be, Chief Inspector Cardinal of the Regional Crime Squad or Chief Constable of the Northumbrian police.

The hotel manager at the George had set aside a room on the first floor where the police could interview witnesses. Grout managed to insert himself into the room, standing quietly at the back while statements were being taken and witnesses interviewed. The constable on duty outside in the corridor had asked to see his ID but had clearly been forewarned of the likelihood that Grout would turn up. He entered as the barman was making a statement, and he remained as a group of other staff, including waitresses and room cleaners were put through their paces. It all became a matter of routine, drudgery even, and Grout became bored. None of the people interviewed seemed to have seen Rigby, or noted anything of significance and Grout began to feel he might have been better employed back at Chesters, who were searching the locality in the hope of finding the murder weapon. It was when the hotel night porter was interviewed however that his interest quickened.

The porter was about sixty years of age, slightly bowed, but elegant in his immaculate if somewhat faded uniform. His grey, thinning hair was swept back neatly, his moustache was trimmed and he showed himself in no way overawed by the situation.

'Now let's get this straight,' Inspector Waters began. 'You were on duty from six in the evening until six next morning?'

'That's right, Inspector. Of course I'd be asleep for a considerable part of that time, because well, there's nothing happening if you know what I mean, once any late comers have gone off to their beds. I check the keys rack, to make sure no one is locked out, but after that I have a snooze. Until dawn. The manager knows about that. He raises no objection. I'm on duty, even so, on hand in case I'm needed.'

Waters tapped the sheet of paper in front of him, in which the porter's statement had been taken earlier by another officer.

'There's just one bit of clarification I want. I'm sure you're aware we've now interviewed all the residents in the hotel, and most of the staff. There's one person we haven't spoken to, a lady who signed the register as...ah...Eileen Grant. There's no record of her checking out, I see.'

The night porter shrugged. 'Far as I know she didn't check out. I spoke to the manager earlier. Seems she paid in advance for her room, so there was no real need I suppose for her to go through any other formalities.'

'No, I suppose not though it's a bit unusual. So you didn't see her leave the hotel?'

'I did not.'

'And you carried her case up to her room when she arrived. How did that come about? You weren't on duty, I imagine.'

The night porter smoothed down the wing of grey hair at the side of his head. 'I was on my way to the stairs when she was going up to her room. I thought it would be the courteous thing to do, to offer assistance.'

Inspector Waters clearly felt it was sufficiently unusual for an off-duty staff member to behave in such a way to press the matter. 'Courteous, hey? Pretty, was she?'

'She was, if you would like to know. But that was nothing to do with it. I been in the business forty years. I believe certain things should be done properly, not because I'm paid to do them, but because it's right to behave like that. My father before me, he...' The old man frowned, realised he was wandering. 'Besides, the case, it was just an overnight bag really, light, probably carrying just flimsy night clothes, that sort of thing. It didn't break my back to help.'

'I see...Anyway, it seems she stayed in her room most of the time.'

'I can't confirm that, Inspector. I wasn't on duty.'

'You stated here you saw the woman a couple of times in the evening.'

The porter nodded. 'I was off duty, but I was around, having a meal, that sort of thing. And I went for my usual evening constitution, across the bridge.'

Inspector Waters leaned forward, elbows on the table between them. 'So precisely where did you see her?'

The porter wrinkled his nose. 'First time I saw her she was standing outside the hotel, on the garden path. I nodded to her when I walked past, and she smiled but said nothing.'

'What was she doing there?'

'Admiring the scenery, I suppose.'

'You suppose?'

The porter shrugged. 'Well she was standing there, looking out towards the river and the road.'

'Not strolling.'

The porter hesitated, then shook his grey head. 'No, just standing there. I suppose, on reflection, you could say she might have been sort of hanging around.'

'Waiting for someone?'

'Who can say?' He thought for a few seconds. 'Maybe she was watching for a car or something, or expected to meet someone. I don't know.'

'When was the next time you saw her?'

'Maybe an hour later, when I was walking back to the hotel after my stroll. That time she was on the terrace. She was casually walking around as though she was enjoying the evening air but again, she could have been keeping an eye on the road and the bridge and the cars, that sort of thing.'

'And you saw her again later?'

'I did. Pretty late it was then. I was going through to the kitchen to pick up the snack they lay out for me and she was in the lounge then. That was about eleven, so she was after a drink I guess.'

'And that was the last you saw of her?' the inspector asked brusquely slipping the statement into a file cover, clearly regarding the interview at an end.

'That it was. But I remember thinking that if things were as they looked she'd—'

'That's fine, thank you.' The inspector interrupted him, tossed the file aside, yawned, flexed his shoulder muscles.

The porter began to rise, his mouth set in a line, probably slightly offended by the manner in which the inspector had cut him off. Grout knew that the inspector would probably be less than pleased if he stepped in but nevertheless he said quietly, 'I'm sorry, sir, but could I have a word?' Before waiting for permission, he spoke to the porter. 'What were you about to say if things were as they looked?'

Inspector Waters was glaring at Grout with steely eyes. But he said in a cold voice, 'Yes, tell us what you were about to say.'

The porter was aware of the sudden drop in temperature between the two officers. But it wasn't his business. 'Well, you see, like I said she was a handsome woman, and not beyond reacting to a man if you know what I mean. So when I saw her there, it occurred to me that he might make a move on her, the way he was trying to catch her eye. I don't know if he managed it, of course, I wasn't aware of any room prowling if you know what I mean...'

'What the hell are you talking about?' the inspector snapped.

'The other guest in the lounge.'

'You made no mention of him earlier'

'Wasn't asked, was I?'

The inspector glanced angrily at Grout and then asked, 'This other guest...who was it?'

'The single gentleman,' the porter said sturdily. 'I mean, there was a group in from Newcastle that night and they were a bit noisy in the bar but it wasn't one of them, though if they'd have seen her I don't doubt one of them would have chanced his arm.'

'The single gentleman,' Waters prompted with a sigh.

'It was Mr Gilbert, of course. The one who found the body down at Chesters, I believe, this morning. He was going into the lounge, looked like he was hoping to join her. I heard later he'd paid for her drink, but what happened after that I don't know. Not surprising though, she was a bonny girl.'

After the porter had left the room the inspector drew the file towards him and stared at it. Bright red spots were burning on his cheeks and he kept his head down when he spoke.

'I did point out you had no standing here, detective sergeant Grout'

'You did, sir.'

'So keep your nose out of it.'

'I—'

'I'd have got around to that bit of information in due course,' Waters announced severely. 'It's our job to carry out these interrogations, not yours, so if are going to stick around, keep your mouth shut. You're an observer, nothing more.'

He stood up, marched across the room, flung open the door and ordered the constable in the corridor to get hold of Paul Gilbert. He came back in, sat down, ignoring Grout and stared at his hands laid flat on the table in front of him. The silence grew around them, edged with hostility. Grout wondered why the inspector was so touchy but he stepped back to lean against the wall when the door finally opened and Paul Gilbert entered.

Grout eyed him curiously.

The man was perhaps thirty five years of age. His features were lean, tanned and his eyes were quick and grey. His hair was sandy in colour, neatly smoothed back and there was a hint of encroaching baldness at the crown of his head. He was a man who was careful about his appearance, grout guessed: he wore an expensive shirt, open at the neck with a silk scarf knotted at the throat. His trousers were pale blue, his shoes pale brown corduroy. Grout felt it was a curiously effeminate outfit. The man's fingers, laced together as he sat down in front of Inspector waters, were slim.

'Mr Paul Gilbert. A photographer, I understand.'

'That's right.'

'And an author.'

'Correct. You have this on file now, don't you?'

The inspector's eyes were hostile as he looked at the silk scarf Gilbert affected. 'These books you write...sex and violence, that sort of thing?'

'Hardly,' Gilbert drawled easily. 'I produce photographic essays, and before you jump to the wrong conclusion they do not include what some describe as art shots.'

'Naked birds, you mean?' the inspector asked insolently.

'If you wish so to describe them. My books are mainly of landscapes. I did a successful production last year based on the West Riding. At present I'm preparing one on Northumberland and Hadrian's Wall. That the reason for my presence at this hotel. I've already told you all this. Or one of your minions, anyway.'

'You are interested in sex, though,' Waters grunted provocatively.

Grout was beginning to think that the inspector's interviewing technique was almost antediluvian and certainly objectionable. Gilbert's back stiffened.

'What on earth do you mean by that remark?'

'Women. You're interested in women.'

Gilbert blinked. 'I have a healthy interest in the other sex, as you probably do, inspector.'

'You married?'

'No.'

'But you have girl friends, is that right?'

'No steady partner, if that's what you mean.' Gilbert's tone hardened. 'What's this got to do with my finding that body at Chesters this morning?'

46

'Don't know yet. But why didn't you tell us about picking up that woman last night in the lounge?'

There was a short silence. At last, Gilbert said, 'I resent the tone of your voice, inspector. I've been asked about, and made a statement concerning what I found this morning. That's the only relevant matter, it seems to me, that can help in your enquiries.'

'Come on, Gilbert, let's have it out in the open. There was a woman here last night. Eileen Grant. You were trying to have it off with her, weren't you?'

'What on earth are you talking about?'

'You paid for her drink, chatted her up. What happened after that?'

"It's none of your damned business!"

Grout felt that Inspector Waters seemed to have touched a raw nerve.

'I repeat, it's none of your business! But I've nothing to conceal. I paid for her drink. We had a chat in the lounge. Then we went to our respective rooms. I didn't see her again after that. She did not appear at breakfast. And that's all I can tell you about her!'

There was anger in his tone, but something else again, Grout suspected. Maybe Gilbert had tried to pick up the Grant woman. He had probably been unsuccessful.

After a moment, Gilbert muttered, 'After we had a drink I went on the terrace. We spoke there for a while. Then she left, I stayed on the terrace. That was it.'

The inspector nodded. Grout felt he should be pressing the matter a little further, less suggestively perhaps, but it seemed that Waters was losing interest in this line of enquiry. He was looking back at the notes taken in Gilbert's earlier interview. Grout would have liked to intervene but had already been told to back off once. He was disinclined to raise the inspector's blood pressure further.

47

'Your statement...' Inspector Waters said. 'You found the body up at Chesters when you were out walking.'

'Yes.'

'You always go for a walk before breakfast?'

Paul Gilbert hesitated slightly. Grout felt the man would have liked to say it was his normal habit, but decided against it.

'No...but, well, I couldn't sleep, Had a bad night.'

'Because of the alcohol you'd drunk?'

Gilbert raised his head disdainfully. 'It was insomnia. I had things on my mind.'

'The woman?'

'I was lying awake, planning my photographic layouts. It can get...obsessive.'

'So there was no particular reason why you wandered in the direction of Chesters?'

'One can obtain interestingly lit shots in the early morning.'

'So you took your camera.'

Gilbert hesitated. 'No.'

Waters looked him directly in the eyes. 'Funny, though. You aren't an habitual morning stroller. You go out, without your camera. And you find a dead man. Pity...you could have taken a shot the newspapers would have paid a bundle for. I think that's something you regret now, hey? But by the way, did you take a shot of that woman, Eileen Gilbert?'

There was a short silence. "I did not," Gilbert said at last.

Once again, Grout had the instinctive feeling there was something Paul Gilbert was holding back. It was nothing he could put his finger on but he felt there was an odd undercurrent, a tension behind the man's words. Grout glanced at Inspector Waters: it seemed the thought had not occurred to him. Grout opened his mouth and then, once again, thought better of it.

'All right Mr Gilbert we'll leave it at that. If you'd be so kind to make a further statement regarding your meeting with Eileen Grant we needn't bother you further.'

Gilbert's chair scraped as he stood up. He stood there for a moment, looking down at the police inspector. 'Why are you so interested in Eileen Grant? Why the questions about her?'

Inspector Waters smiled thinly. 'Just following up on anything of interest, Mr Gilbert. Just make the statement. Add perhaps what you talked about, that sort of thing.'

'She said little. We just talked about my work.'

'There you are then. That tells us something, doesn't it? She's interested in photography!'

Gilbert scowled. 'It was just a casual conversation. But what has she got to do with all this...business?'

He could not bring himself to mention the dead man at Chesters.

Inspector Waters gathered up his papers. His tone was cool. 'We don't know yet. The fact is, this lady friend of yours, she up and left early this morning, it seems. Sort of...disappeared.'

Chief Inspector James Cardinal arrived in Newcastle that evening. Rooms had been booked for him and grout at the Turks head Hotel. Grout met the senior officer in the bar before dinner. Cardinal ordered drinks for them both, and after a brief hesitation told the barman to put the tab on his room. Grout guessed the hesitation was due to Cardinal's hope that Grout would dig into his own pocket for the drinks. It was a game of cat and mouse that grout had become accustomed to playing: he knew that if he waited, Cardinal would give in. It was a minor triumph but one he enjoyed.

'I had a long talk with the Chief Constable,' Cardinal said. He sipped his Newcastle Brown and pulled a lugubrious face. 'Strong stuff this. I spent the afternoon with him at Ponteland and put him in the picture. It's what I expected: I had to work on him a while before he agreed we could continue an involvement in the investigation into Rigby's murder. He says his own people have plenty on their plates anyway.'

Grout had little doubt Inspector Waters would be less than pleased.

'We can use the lab facilities up at Gosforth," Cardinal continued. "Any other help we need, we can just ask for it.'

'I doubt if the lower ranks will go along with that willingly,' Grout observed.

'Touchy, are they? Well, it's to be expected, I suppose. So your visit to Chesters wasn't all wine and roses.'

'Truculence was in the air.'

'Truculence.' Cardinal registered that he was impressed by the choice of word. Then he grinned. He was in an expansive mood. He could remember that not so long ago Grout had been a member of a provincial force and would have bitterly resented the entry of the Regional Crime Squad to his manor. Shows how situations can alter feelings, he concluded to himself.

'So where do you go from here?' Cardinal asked.

'There are several questions I want to ask witnesses...they'll have dispersed so I'll have to chase them up.'

'Legwork's good for you, lad,' Cardinal said approvingly. 'Get you away from those books you stick your head into. You're a copper not a lawyer. Anyway, fill me in with what you've got.'

Grout did so, telling him what had happened at Chesters and at the George Hotel.

'You think this girl—'

'Eileen Grant. At least, that's how she registered herself at the hotel. Could be an assumed name, of course.'

'She's possibly tied up in the murder?'

'That's going a bit too far, sir, at the moment. But it's a possibility. All this hanging around outside the hotel...could be she was waiting for Rigby, or even for the man who killed him.'

Cardinal grimaced. 'Bit too far for my money.'

'She left the hotel without checking out.'

Cardinal nodded, frowned. 'You think this Gilbert feller has more to tell us?'

Grout nodded.

'I'd like to have another word with him. There's something he was holding back. But I don't know what, and it may not be important. Still...'

They were silent for a little while. Cardinal employed himself by steadily emptying his glass. Then he stared at it, raised his eyes to Grout, and scowled until Grout took the message.

'Same again, sir?'

'No,' he replied, to Grout's relief. The relief was short-lived. 'No, I'll have a Jameson this time. Double. I'm partial to Irish whisky, even if I have no love for the Irish themselves. All that peat.'

Grout went to the bar and obtained the drinks, settling for a half of Newcastle Brown for himself. When he returned, Cardinal said, 'Leave this woman Grant to me. We've got her description: I'll get it circulated. The address she gave on the register might not check out, but we'll see, and as for the photographer Gilbert, let him stew a few days. Don't push him. If he's got more to tell us pressure right now might make him dig in his heels but if he's left alone, cool down, thinks he's clear a bit of verbal hammering might cause him to collapse. That's called psychology, Grout.'

Cod psychology, Grout thought to himself.

'Then there's the other question to consider.'

'The museum?'

'Exactly that,' Cardinal nodded. 'We need to find out why it got broken into. Was it Rigby himself? And if so what the hell was he after? Apart from which, what was a fairly well-provided art thief, working for my old friend Clifford, doing out at Chesters in the first place?'

'He was supposed to have been on his way to London for the meeting.'

Cardinal sipped his whisky with an air of satisfaction, partly because it was a Jameson, and partly because he had not paid for it himself. 'I bet Clifford's fingers are all over this business. I'd bet my bottom dollar on it. But what I can't figure is what would be in the museum at Chesters to pull Rigby there, never mind why he got clobbered for his pains. Was Rigby obeying orders from his boss, or did he get hammered because he was striking out on his own? You find out, Grout, and who knows? I might even put in your case for promotion.'

That old carrot again, Grout thought. 'I think my first task will be to have a word with the guy who leads the University Survey group who've been working at the museum. The curator reckons they'll know the contents more closely than he does. I'll begin by having a word with the head of the archaeological section in the department. Professor Godfrey.'

Cardinal frowned. 'Godfrey? I fancy I've come across that name somewhere.' Then he recollected: his wife watched popular television programmes about archaeology, and often drooled about a professor called Godfrey. 'He wouldn't be that TV chap, would he?'

'Don't know, sir.'

'That's right,' Cardinal said sourly. 'Law not archaeology is your thing. God knows what you hope to get out of all that study. Still, it'll be up your street, swanning around the university corridors, hob-nobbing with those young oiks and their stuck-up teachers, dons, whatever they call themselves. Did I ever tell you I never went to university, Grout?'

Mentally, Grout groaned. He suspected Cardinal was going to talk about the University of Life.

'I'm a graduate of the University of Life, me.'

Cardinal rose to his feet, a tall, slim man with the beginnings of a middle-aged paunch. Two inches shorter, younger, thicker in the body and slower in his movements Grout scrambled to his feet. Cardinal eyed him carefully.

'You knew I was going to say that, didn't you, Grout?'

Grout hesitated, then shrugged non-committally.

'Smart arse,' Cardinal said and led the way from the bar towards the dining room. 'You can buy the wine.'

CHAPTER FOUR

Detective Sergeant Grout was never quite certain about his relationship with Chief Inspector Cardinal.

The DCI had arranged for him to join the Regional Crime Squad, presumably because he had been impressed by the work Grout had put in when they had been thrown together during an illegal immigrant case in Bradford. He suspected Cardinal had a grudging respect for the fact that Grout had a certain fluency in Urdu, which had come in useful on that occasion; Grout also suspected that Cardinal, for all his sneering comments about the studies he was pursuing towards a degree in Law, quietly approved of the fact he was trying to extend his qualifications.

On the other hand Cardinal also seemed to put as many obstacles in his way as he possibly could, restricting the time he had available to study—albeit while rightly insisting that his full time job with the Squad must come first. But it all led to a confusion in Grout's mind: he could not work out just what Cardinal really felt about him. As a colleague, and as a man.

What was certainly clear was the fact that Cardinal was determined to get the last ounce of effort out of Grout in the carrying out of his duties.

His appointment to meet Professor Godfrey at the university was quickly made. When he arrived at the Professor's office he recognised him immediately as a man who had made frequent television appearances even though Grout would have been unable to identify the programmes in which the academic had appeared.

'Ah, yes,' Godfrey said, nodding his head and laughing in a somewhat embarrassed fashion which Grout felt was a little theatrical, 'it's one of the problems associated with the media spotlight. Being recognised in the street and yet being taken for some other celebrity—not that I really regard myself as a celebrity! In addition, I've come to realise that the academic world being what it is, one loses a certain amount of credibility among colleagues if one appears too often. A panel game for morons and a tutorial or lecture presentation before some of the best brains in university circles...some people regard these as occupations that are, shall we say, mutually exclusive.'

Godfrey was a few inches taller than Grout, broad-shouldered, immaculately dressed in an elegantly cut grey suit. His features were finely-chiselled, good-humoured and as he spoke he leant forward as though wishing to build personal bridges with the person he was talking to. His brown hair curled thickly on the top of his head but at the temples there was a frosting of silver. Women would find this man attractive and television would enhance his insistently sincere gaze. He was reputed to receive a considerable fan mail for his Sunday afternoon cultural programmes and the inanities of the panel game he chaired on Tuesday evenings would seem to fix millions in their armchairs. He was unmarried and his secretary clearly adored him, as did many of the middle-aged women who were addicted to his appearances. As they sat in the Senior Common Room Godfrey offered Grout a drink. Grout refused: he had a suspicion it might be sherry. Courteously, Godfrey refrained from calling for a drink for himself.

'I don't get too much hassle from my colleagues at the university here,' Godfrey announced, crossing one leg over the other as he settled back into his leather armchair. 'A certain amount of chaffing goes on, naturally: it's understandable. The thing is, as long as one maintains a reasonable academic reputation with published works, it's possible to keep the critics at bay. I get a few snide remarks in the press thrown at me from time to time, but one must develop a thick skin to ward off such gnat bites, don't you agree?'

Grout had never appeared on television, and did not expect to do so. But he agreed with the comment. It was d difficult to do otherwise with this charming and easy-mannered man.

'I understand one of your published works concerns Chesters' Grout said.

'Oh, it wasn't just about Chesters,' the professor replied swiftly. 'It ranged across the whole raft of reasons for the building of the original Wall, the legions that built it, the pinnacle of its utility, its gradual abandonment and decay...no, the book did not concentrate merely on Chesters. On the other hand, you probably refer to the slighter book on Chesters itself, that was merely an extract from the major work...there was a local print run that was quite successful. I have a copy or two in my room: I'll let you have a signed copy if you would like one.'

Non-committally, Grout replied, 'You'll have heard about the murder that was recently committed up at Chesters.'

'My dear chap' Godfrey spread his hands theatrically, 'I was one of the first people local television contacted to obtain some background and local colour. They didn't actually use me personally in the presentation but...well, the event has set things buzzing in the north, hasn't it? So romantic, after all: a murder at such an historic site.'

There had been nothing romantic about the flies buzzing around Rigby's smashed skull, but Grout did not give voice to the thought. Godfrey smiled his easy, understanding smile.

'You would see things in quite a different light, of course. But you must remember we all have our personal perspectives. As an historian I am always tempted to take the long term view, place matters in their historical context. My public career, enhanced and perhaps, I admit, somewhat twisted by the demands of the media upon my time, has emerged from the romantic mists that antiquity bestows upon what many regard as the mundane. Of course, this has brought me considerable financial rewards and allowed me to build up my own personal collection of interesting artefacts of historical value. But in short, I believe in the drama of history.'

Codswallop, Grout thought.

'Even yesterday's history,' Godfrey continued thoughtfully. 'Which is really why you wanted to talk with me, so, enough inconsequential chatter. In what manner may I be able to help you?'

Grout was becoming somewhat irritated by the hint of condescension in Godfrey's tone and the rather portentous phrasing he used. Bluntly, he said, 'I want to hear about your Survey Group, and the work you've done at Chesters.'

'Really?' Godfrey seemed surprised. 'I can't see what my little group would have to do with a murdered man up at Chesters.'

'General enquiries,' Grout grunted.

Godfrey twisted his mouth in a grimace of consideration. 'Well, let's see, I formed the group about four years ago. Since I took over as head of the Antiquities Department here, things have progressed rather well, even if I do say so myself. After I obtained my professorial chair and published my monograph on the Wall the television work started and a number of research students were consequently attracted to the department. I suppose the publicity drew them in, and perhaps the hope that they also might make the odd appearance on the box. Interesting, isn't it? What people will do to attain their brief fame...'

'The work you did at Chesters,' Grout reminded the self-satisfied academic.

'Ah yes, well, it seemed to me it would be worthwhile to introduce new students to the beauty and thrill of archaeology by letting them handle and deal with items that were stored at Chesters. It allowed them to develop instincts for dating, to make allowance for the feel of history under their clumsy hands, to inculcate in them an understanding of workmanship and time and the endeavours of men who once trod these hills but have now vanished into dust...' Godfrey's glance fixed on Grout's. He became aware of the frown on the detective sergeant's brow. He shrugged. 'The idea was simple and, I admit, not new. It helped the students develop documentation, identify locations, look for signs of archaeological interest, and took them into the realms of historical records, parish registers, classical accounts...in reality, I had a fairly catholic view of the activity of the group. Anything that might add to our store of knowledge, and enhance the student understanding of history, it was all grist to our mill.'

'Your students worked at the museum at Chesters.'

'Naturally. I don't imagine you'll wish to interview any of them about it, however. They'll have nothing to impart which I can't cover. I keep a close eye on all that's gone on in the museum. It's a matter of responsibility, don't you know?' Abruptly, he rose and smiled. 'But you never know, do you?' He gestured towards the door. 'Come. I'll take you down, introduce you to Dobson.'

Aaron Dobson turned out to be a somewhat pimply young man who was prematurely bald. He was probably no more than twenty five years of age but his pate shone: Grout was reminded of a pink billiard ball.

He was a rather nervous young man who kept stroking his eyebrows as though assuring himself they were still there: his glance was quick and agitated, his hands rarely still. Godfrey introduced him as the student leader of the group: Grout assumed it would have been on account of his intellectual abilities rather than his leadership qualities, for Dobson seemed to be in an almost constant state of terror in his struggle to face the world of his choosing.

'Yeah, that's right, we've been working up at Chesters on and off for a couple of years now,' Dobson stated, 'It's not had a high priority in the department, I mean, it's the kind of resource we can use from time to time, particularly with the youngsters who come into the department.' He glanced nervously at Professor Godfrey. 'It can get pretty boring from time to time.'

Godfrey smiled indulgently.

'Do you have a catalogue of the contents at the museum storeroom?' Grout asked. 'The curator seemed a bit vague about it: he didn't really seem to know what was stored there.'

Dobson gave his eyebrow a little tug.

'We do, yeah, because of the young students we have working there. I mean, you got to keep tabs on things, don't you? There's a handout we made up for the Ministry of Works, though our stuff is more detailed, and some of the items we list we're not sure about, dating, provenance, that sort of thing. You see, the problem is—'

'What I'm really interested in,' Grout interrupted, daunted by the likely flow of irrelevant information Dobson was likely to produce, 'is just a list of the storeroom contents.'

Dobson blinked. His fingers wandered up to his eyebrow again, but he then restrained himself. 'The stuff in the basement, yeah. Apart from our general list I don't think there's much we can do to help.'

'You haven't a complete catalogue?' Grout asked in surprise. 'Neither you nor the curator—'

'Well, it's been kind of low priority, you understand. Some of the stuff has been identified, written up, because if we have a student who's specialising the chances are he or she will have done some rooting around. The storeroom contents, well, we've all been involved in that but the general view is that there's not much down there which is of significant interest. I mean, if it was, it wouldn't be down there, if you know what I mean. It'd be upstairs, wouldn't it?'

Grout sighed. He had the feeling he was wading around in thick mud, getting nowhere. Nevertheless, he had to admit Dobson was probably right. So the question remained: why was the museum broken into, by Rigby or his killer? If nothing appeared to have been taken, why had anyone bothered to break in?

'On the other hand,' Dobson murmured, creasing his brow thoughtfully, 'it could be I'm not exactly right.'

'What's that?' Grout asked, puzzled.

'Well, like I said, we been working at Chesters for a few years and the team's changed over that time, as students have come in, moved off, taken up other projects, so when I spoke I was thinking about the present team, of course.'

'Of course' Grout repeated, not understanding what Dobson was talking about.

'I said a moment ago, we each had sort of special interests, the ones who worked at Chesters. There was Phil Proud, of course. His special interest was thirteenth century. Not just Britain. European stuff as well.'

'Phil Proud.'

'That's the man. He was on the team a year or so ago before he moved on. I seem to recall that when he was rooting around in the basement he did some cataloguing. And more than that: he seemed to spend more time there than we would have expected.'

'Are you suggesting he might have made a more detailed analysis of the stuff down there than you or the curator might have done?'

'Something like that,' Dobson replied, somewhat defensively.

'Where can I find him?' Grout asked.

'No idea. I mean, he's no longer at the university. He sort of got thrown out.' Dobson grimaced, then corrected himself. 'Not thrown out exactly. I mean, he was awarded his MA and off he went, although there was an expectation he would have been taken on as a researcher. But there was some sort of kerfuffle, I don't know, bit of trouble about his thesis, he lost it or something, but it was Professor Godfrey who pulled the rabbit out of the hat.'

'How do you mean' Grout asked, puzzled.

'The Prof fought Proud's corner. He pushed his case. The Prof's a good guy, you know? He argued with the Senate and got them to award the degree even though something had happened to the thesis. But the Prof can tell you all about that. Maybe he can even tell you where Proud ended up. Sorry I can't be of more help, man.'

There was something almost sixty-ish about Dobson's manner of speaking. Perhaps he was fated to remain in the time warp that was the university department of Archaeology.

Professor Godfrey lounged back in his chair, flicked a spot of lint from his cuff and smiled at Grout as he waved him to a seat in his small office.

'Yes, I thought there wouldn't be a great deal of assistance you would be able to get from the department staff: you must realise, Sergeant, that all our staff exist in their own little worlds. They are academics, or budding academics, and they are obsessed with their fields of specialism. Little interests them beyond that, other than the usual things like beer and girls. The single ones, anyway. Though I suspect the married ones also have those external....well, maybe I shouldn't go there. No, their lives are largely dictated by the range of their work: exhibits at a museum, learned writings, ancient documents...they don't find much to interest them in an out of the way storeroom.'

Grout sat down on the chair facing the Professor, after first removing several books and placing them on the floor beside the chair. Sunlight lanced through the rather dirty window and he was aware of the distant sound of traffic funnelling up from the Haymarket. He remained silent for a little while.

'So is there anything else we can help you with?' Professor Godfrey queried.

'Dobson mentioned a former student of yours, by the name of Phil Proud.'

Grout could not be entirely certain, but he felt he detected a certain change in Godfrey's hitherto easy manner. His glance flickered around the room as he seemed to hesitate, collecting his thoughts, marshalling his thought processes. He rose to his feet, turned to look out of the window, peering through the grime to the streets below. 'Philip Proud.' There was a certain hesitancy in his tone.

'Dobson reckoned Proud spent more time in the Chesters storeroom that was usual. Does that mean Proud might have developed a catalogue of some sort?'

Godfrey shrugged, turned back from the window, settling himself once more in his chair. He shuffled some papers on his desk in front of him, almost absent-mindedly. 'That may well be so, though it's something that hasn't previously come to my attention. In fact, I'm somewhat surprised to hear of it. I mean, Chesters was a Roman fort, the antiquities discovered there, they were almost all artefacts from the Roman period, some valuable, some run of the mill, so to speak. But Proud's interests were related to a study of the thirteenth century in Europe, that disastrous epoch when so much collapsed, values were questioned, religion and superstition and raw ambitions raged out of control in civilised societies...if you could call them civilised. Rooting around Chesters would have been a waste of time for young Proud. Maybe that's why he ended up the way he did.'

Grout seemed to detect an irritated disapproval in the professor's tone.

'Weren't you his supervisor?'

Godfrey spread his hands in an ineffectual gesture. 'Of course, but one can't keep track...and in many ways it's important that students seek their own byways to reach the goals they aspire to. You feel I should have directed him more closely? Maybe that's true. But one has only so much time, and there are one's own interests to consider...'

Like television appearances, Grout thought.

'But let me be clear. Proud was a good student. And perhaps I set my standards too high. He was good, but in the long run I suppose I have to admit that I found his work...disappointing.'

'Why was that?'

'I hesitate to explain. It's a long story'

'Give me a summary'

Godfrey grimaced, took a deep breath. 'If you wish. Philip Proud came to the university to read for his first degree. History. He took a First and when he asked if I would take him on as a research student while he read for his Master's, by thesis, I agreed. He seemed good material. The field he wished to undertake research into, well, it wasn't my specialist area, but there are always colleagues one can refer to, and he seemed bright, so I agreed.''

'What particular field was he interested in?'

'Mediaeval Italy. Firenze and the Borgias. Blood-letting and murder. Power struggles and the explosion of mediaeval art. All very exciting and romantic. I was impressed by his enthusiasm. There was not a lot I could do to direct his studies, but I did what I could to help.'

'Even when he got into some kind of trouble with his thesis?'

Godfrey raised an eyebrow, and stared at Grout. Then he nodded. 'Of course. Dobson would have mentioned that.' The professor gave a reluctant shrug. 'It was not exactly trouble. More, it was some kind of falling off with his work ethic in the first instance. He worked well enough at the beginning, indeed, for most of the year but then somehow he seemed to slacken off. He missed a few of his tutorials with me, was absent for a period from the campus. I cornered him at one point, asked him what was going on, if there was a problem I could help deal with. I got the impression it was probably a personal matter...the usual thing, a girl in the background.' Godfrey smiled ruefully. 'We've all been there, isn't that so?' When Grout made no reply, Godfrey went on, 'So there wasn't much I could do. And to be honest, even though he was, well, not slacking, but being less committed, wheat I saw of his written work was well up to the standard I would have expected, and called for. In fact his raw thesis was good. It needed polishing, of course, and some of his references required further elucidation and support, put on the whole it was a sound piece of research and well worth publication. Not that it was ever published, unfortunately.'

'Why was that?'

Godfrey was silent for a little while. His fingers teased at one of the documents on the desk in front of him. 'It seems he lost his thesis.'

'Lost it?'

'It got destroyed, burned...the point was he couldn't present the final version to the Senate. By carelessness, or whatever it was, he was throwing away his chance of obtaining his degree, and he seemed to wish to offer no reasonable explanation for it all.'

'Did he explain how the thesis was lost?'

'Not really. Or I should say, not convincingly. I always had a suspicion that he was telling me only half the story, stepping away from the truth. He came up with some vague litany of events, how he'd left his rooms unlocked, how other students may have raided it as some sort of prank; drunk, they trashed his place and in the process his thesis went missing. He alluded vaguely to certain other students with who he was not popular but there was nothing concrete to go on, it seems the manuscript got burned, and—'

'Did he not have a copy on his computer?'

Godfrey eyed him, eyebrows raised. 'Ah, well, it seems that his laptop, which contained the details of his research and all his references, that also got trashed. Or disappeared. I can't quite recall the details.'

'But you thought he wasn't telling you the whole story. Did you have any thoughts about what really might have happened?'

Godfrey wrinkled his brow, smoothed one hand carefully along the side of his head. 'One doesn't wish to enquire too deeply into personal matters. But I came to the conclusion it was all about the...attachment he had developed. The girl he was dating, living with, I don't know, it wasn't for me to pry, my guess was that they had had a violent quarrel, something had gone wrong, she trashed his manuscript and maybe made off with, or threw his laptop in the Tyne, I don't know...Perhaps he hadn't been given her the attention she thought she deserved. Perhaps there was something more serious. Maybe she wasn't a well-balanced young woman. Who knows? Not my business.'

'But the upshot was a year's work was destroyed, and he had no thesis to present.'

Godfrey sighed. 'There were a few notes. And I had my own notes from the sessions we had together, when I was supervising his work he was a foolish young man. He should have taken rather more precautions, in my view. I mean, it was all so...irresponsible.'

'But he was finally awarded his MA...by your efforts, I understand,' Grout murmured.

Godfrey shrugged again and was silent for a little while. Grout waited. He thought about the influx of students to Godfrey's department and realised that the professor's treatment of Philip Proud would be symptomatic of the close regard the man had for his students. He would be popular for his extrovert manner and his television appearances but they would probably also respect him for the interest he took in their academic welfare...and perhaps their personal lives.

'After he was awarded his MA, did Proud take up an academic appointment?' Grout asked.

'Did he hell!' Godfrey snapped and Grout realised that there might be reasons other those mentioned for Godfrey's disappointment in Philip Proud. He had helped the young man, nurtured his talent, assisted him towards the award of his MA in difficult circumstances, but there was something needling Godfrey about Philip Proud.

'So what happened to him after he left the university?'

'Do you know York?' Godfrey asked abruptly.

'Fairly well.'

'You'll know the Shambles then.'

'Most people do.' The Shambles was the mediaeval street right in the centre of York with its overhanging windows, narrow street, lurching, crowded houses beloved by tourists. No longer the habitat of sellers of meat it remained perhaps the most perfectly preserved mediaeval street in Britain, and was much beloved by tourists.

'If you walk into the Shambles from the lower end, that's St Hilary's end, you'll soon come across a small bookshop. If you were to put something completely out of character in that beautiful street you'd install Philip Proud there. In pursuit of Venus. Selling cheap, salacious, paperback books mainly for the erotic trade.'

His tones were edged with disgust. Grout could not be certain whether the disgust came from Proud's involvement with eroticism or simply with the book trade itself.

'So how did he come to set up there?'" Grout asked.

'I understand he received some sort of legacy from a deceased aunt, but I've no idea how much it was, or indeed how he manages to keep his head above water financially, because I don't believe there's much trade down there. From what I hear the place is closed half the time anyway, and in the present state the book trade finds itself in... You know, if he had a legacy like that he could have done something useful with it, extended his learning, gone to Italy to do further research but instead of that the young fool deserted academia for the salacious end of the commercial world! Pornographic literature...and in the Shambles, at that!'

It was clear to Grout that Godfrey regarded Proud's offence as even more heinous than allowing his precious thesis to have been destroyed. Grout was silent, making no attempt to sympathise, feeling that Proud was a young man making his own decisions for his own reasons: he was not to be bound by the desires and dictates of his older mentor. He glanced up and was surprised to see that Godfrey was staring at him with a half smile on his face. It suggested to Grout that Godfrey was quite capable of self-analysis and was feeling slightly abashed at having expressed himself so forcibly.

'You must think I'm somewhat ivory-tower, and perhaps a certain ...Victorian in my attitudes?'

'I think you were understandably disappointed, Professor Godfrey.'

'Yet who am I, really, to offer criticism?' Godfrey spread his hands wide in a somewhat theatrical gesture. 'After all, there are those I'm certain would rush to argue that I have prostituted my knowledge and talents to the ravening beast that is television. I suppose that's the trouble, really: university professors do live in a somewhat narrow world, and have difficulty seeing the wider issues...such as the need to earn a living. Maybe that's what drove Proud, though I can't believe he's making much success of his life on the road he's chosen for himself...'

He nodded, moved towards the door, intimating the interview was at an end as far as he was concerned. 'I forget that I was once young too,' he murmured. 'But then, traditionally, all professors are forgetful, aren't they?'

So are detective sergeants, from time to time, Grout considered as he made his way down Blackett Street, away from the University. He had forgotten to ask

Professor Godfrey for the loan of his monograph on
Chesters Fort.

CHAPTER FIVE

Cardinal received Grout's report in silence.

His lean, ascetic features remained impassive but Grout was in no doubt of the chief inspector's disapproval. He stumbled to the end of his account, stubbornly defiant in his tone of voice as he realised the extent of Cardinal's displeasure. Cardinal fixed a cold, contemptuous glance on the uncomfortable detective sergeant. 'So, you had an enjoyable time fannying around, then?'

'I don't understand, sir.'

Cardinal allowed himself a thin smile: there was no warmth in it.

'As far as I can gather you've been having a pleasant time swanning around York chatting with a professor and a student while the rest of us have been keeping our noses to the grindstone. What your buggering about with academia has to do with the investigation we're carrying out, I haven't the faintest idea. Perhaps you could elucidate the point for me. Is that the right kind of academic phrase?'

Grout's chin came up stubbornly.

'Things might get a bit more clear when I've been allowed to interview this man Proud, sir.'

'Allowed?' Cardinal's eyes widened in mock surprise. 'Seems to me you're wandering off on a frolic of your own with or without permission! As for this man Proud, you're not seriously suggesting you waste time talking to him about his life style, his bloody thesis on mediaeval Italy, or whatever else you want to have a chat about. It's not that you have a leaning towards dirty books, is it?'

Grout was annoyed. He felt he didn't deserve that kind of crack. Doggedly, he said, 'I just feel he might

70

be able to help us with regard to why the Chesters storeroom was broken into.'

'I thought it just contained run of the mill stuff. So what will he have to tell us?'

'Until I speak to him, sir, how can we know?'

Grout sensed it was a standoff. But Cardinal was not the man to admit defeat. He shook his head sadly. 'You know, Grout, I sometimes despair about you. I can't see how Proud will be able to help us in the Rigby killing, or connections to Clifford, or anything else arising out of this bloody mess. We don't even know whether Proud did any cataloguing in that storeroom, and even if he did, you tell me it was over a year ago. I just don't see what possible use...'

Cardinal paused. He was tempted to tell Grout that he should terminate the enquiry into the storeroom contents immediately. He should be concentrating on discovering who had killed Rigby rather than messing about with a break-in at the museum which might have no connection whatsoever to Rigby. They didn't even know if anything had even been taken from the site...or why Rigby was there in the first place. He was tempted...but he hesitated.

It was not that Cardinal thought Grout might be right, and on a useful track: he was fairly certain the sergeant was on a wild goose chase. On the other hand, since Grout had been working with him in the Regional Crime Squad Cardinal had become aware that Grout possessed a certain advantage over his superior officer: he was a man to whom things happened, and his mind was of the kind that could leap an abyss of indecision and reach surprising, and accurate conclusions. It was called flair, he supposed.

He grunted. He knew he was a meticulous, plodding sort of copper—the results he achieved were usually a consequence of long, arduous, slogging drudgery. But

Grout was of the kind to whom coincidence and accident were bedfellows. And he profited accordingly. After all, it was why Cardinal had recruited him in the first instance. It was why he felt he needed Grout. They made a good combination: cardinal to restrain Grout from his wilder flights; Grout to inject the unusual and unexpected into Cardinal's routine investigations.

The uneasy silence was finally broken by Grout clearing his throat nervously. 'Have we got anything yet on the girl who was staying at the hotel, sir?'

Cardinal shook his head. 'Nothing yet. Her description has been circulated and I've got two men checking on likely female contacts of Rigby's. It seems,' he added sourly, 'they are rather numerous. Rigby should have been a sailor, in my view.'

'How have they managed to check?'

'Apart from usual known acquaintances, the keys we found in Rigby's pocket were linked to a flat in Gosforth. Expensive place too, more than I could bloody afford. Anyway, there was some useful stuff there—'

'Anything tying him in with Clifford?'

'Rigby wasn't stupid enough to leave anything of that kind lying around. But there was stuff he was in the process of getting rid of, it seems. Papers had been dumped in the incinerator in the basement, but there were odd sheets that didn't get completely burned. Forensic had a crack at them and they think they'll manage to piece together some information from it all.'

'But you mentioned women friends.'

'Didn't get that from the papers that were dumped. No, much simpler. A diary in a bedroom drawer. Maybe he didn't think it was that important, or just forgot about it before he essayed forth into the night to get his skull crushed up at Chesters. No, the girls were noted there. Some of them hookers, we think; some personal friends. My guess is we'll find most of them are...or were, rather...in gainful employment with Rigby.'

Grout frowned. 'So we might find the missing Miss Grant in there somewhere.'

'Under another name, maybe. She's not turned up yet.'

'But what about the papers he was dumping? What importance did they have? And why get rid of them so suddenly?'

Cardinal shrugged. 'Something was panicking Rigby. He wanted to clear some stuff, get rid of information, and then get off to Chesters. We don't know why. And was it because of the meeting in London, or because of its cancellation? Who knows, at this stage.'

'But you think it's all linked to Clifford's operation.'

'I'm hoping so. I'm hoping we'll be able to find a connection between the murder of Rigby, and the whole business that Clifford's been running. So far, we can't be certain: this might be a gangland killing, or a personal matter, and to date wc've no whisper from the Met that there is a link, but then, they're not even sure that Clifford is still in their area. He seems to have gone to ground, while his other agents have also been scurrying for cover.'

'Sinking ship.'

Cardinal scowled. 'I don't think it'll be as good as that: no, the rats will be diving overboard because they've been told to do so. Yes, maybe Clifford's finding the heat too much for him; he might be wanting to close down some of his activities. But I have a feeling...'

'Sir?'

'Something else is going down. It's just my gut rumbling probably, but I feel he's just closing down temporarily because he's got some other iron he wants to heat up in the fire. But what that might be...'

Cardinal rose and walked across to the map he had placed on his wall. He stared at it moodily for a little while, then sighed, turned back to Grout.

'First thing, we check on these girls. If we're lucky, one of them will turn out to be the woman at the George. We need the answer to one question from her: was she waiting for Rigby or was she waiting for the man who killed him? And why did she go to ground so swiftly? What has she got to hide?'

That's three questions, Grout thought, not one. He did not say so.

'And then there's this photographer character: Paul Gilbert. I want a check done on him. I've been reading the notes on his interview and the statement he gave to the guys at Ponteland HQ. I'm not happy about them. As you said, it must have been clumsy, that inspector doesn't have the techniques...Anyway, I think we need to have another chat with Mr Gilbert. We've got his address: he lives at Beverley, in the East Riding. I want you to take a car, Grout, and go pick him up. We'll use the York office to have a chat with him. I'll join you there this afternoon.'

Grout hesitated, opened his mouth, then closed it again. Cardinal scowled.

'And since you're going to be near York, all right, I suppose we might as well let you indulge your passion for the academic—or is it the pornographic? You can do a detour, call in and go see this bookseller you're so keen to interview.' Cardinal shook his head disapprovingly. 'But I'll be more than surprised if Proud is of any use to us.'

Since his meeting with Cardinal was not due to take place until late afternoon Grout decided to call on Philip Proud before he went out to Beverley to pick up Paul Gilbert.

He left his car in the station car park and walked across the bridge and through the streets until he reached the Shambles. Proud's shop was just a short distance from St Hilary's and Grout found it immediately, but made no attempt to enter; instead, he wandered along the Shambles for the sheer pleasure of taking in its mediaeval ambience. He found himself in agreement with the views of Professor Godfrey when he returned: Philip Proud's commercial venture was hardly in keeping with the street itself. The narrow leaded windows of the bookshop were packed with paperbacks with salacious titles of the kind that would once have been seized by the police years earlier, as much for their failure to deliver what the covers promised, as much as anything else.

Grout entered the shop and found himself in a small room, the shelves being browsed among by several middle-aged gentlemen and a few prurient youngsters of school age. No-one seemed intent on buying: they were there for a thrill they were unlikely to achieve, and the boys should have been at school anyway, but Grout wasn't interested in doing anything about that. He made his way along towards the back of the room, glancing vacantly at some of the more lurid titles. Proud had spent a fair amount of money on his stock, that was clear. Much of it, in Grout's view, would have been wasted.

He became aware of someone standing behind him. He began to turn when someone spoke quietly. 'If you're at all interested, sir, we have some rather more fascinating material in the next room.'

Grout stared at the young man who had addressed him. He guessed he was in his early twenties, thin, dark-suited, sporting a pink shirt, floral tie and fashionably-framed spectacles. His hair was dark and neatly combed, and a hint of a moustache graced his upper lip. His eyes were almost china-blue, and innocently frank. Grout supposed it was one way of persuading the punters that all was on the level.

Grout nodded, saying nothing; the young man took it for acquiescence and gestured towards the back of the shop. He led the way. The room beyond was narrow and low-ceilinged; it was also rather dim. Grout stared at the shelves ranged around the room: there were books on flagellation, sadism, masochism, bondage, and a collection of Victorian bodice-rippers were grouped in one corner. The young man turned, smiled shyly. 'Of course, if you're interested in something even more sophisticated—'

'I'm a police officer.'

'Oh, sod it!'

The two stared at each other. The blue eyes had changed; the professional innocence was still there but emoting chagrin and embarrassment. The young man seemed to regard Grout's presence as an unfair intrusion; he was disturbed at his failure to recognise danger when it loomed up in front of him.

'I can usually spot the fuzz at a distance of half a mile.'

His tone was aggrieved. Grout shrugged. 'I'm not too happy myself, being taken for one of the dirty mac brigade.'

'Go no further,' the bookseller interrupted, holding up a warning hand. 'There is nothing harmful in pornography and it's a mistake to classify all readers of erotica as semi-deranged, hole in the corner, sexual fanatics. I like it myself, in fact,' he added rather gloomily. 'Sex, that is. I don't really go in for erotica.'

'You sell it,' Grout challenged.

'It's a living.'

'You're Philip Proud, I imagine.'

The blue eyes took on an expression of surprise. 'How did you know my name? I don't use it in this business. Fallacies Unlimited. I would have used a different spelling but that would have appeared too in-your-face, and advertising might have been a problem. With objections from the rest of the Shambles, I would guess, too.'

'And you deserted the academic world for this stuff.'

'That sounds like an echo from someone else I know.'

'Is there somewhere we can talk? Other than here.'

'Erotica makes you uncomfortable. I can understand that. But it's only a part of life.' Proud wrinkled his nose. 'I have a room upstairs that serves as an office. We can go there.'

Grout looked back to the room they had left. 'What about your customers? Aren't you in danger of their stealing something if you're not around to watch?'

'I know most of them...apart from the kids. And they're not really purchasers, or thieves. They just like to stand there, read a while, dream, mentally masturbate...Would you like to follow me?'

Proud led the way to a narrow staircase that took them to the upper floor. The office they entered was neat, and on the desk was a monitor that gave a view of the main room below and the front door. Proud was not as casual as he tried to make out: he could see what was going on downstairs while he was up here in the office.

'So,' Proud said as he perched one thigh on the edge of the desk, 'You from the vice squad, or what?'

'I've no interest in the tools of your trade.'

'No interest in erotica? So why are you here?'

'I'd like to talk to you about your thesis.'

There was a short, puzzled silence. 'It did make a few comments about some of the statuary held in respectable Roman homes, but there was nothing in it about erotomania or anything like that.'

'I told you: your books don't interest me. I'm simply interested in why you deserted the academic life and—'

'Godfrey! He knows something about this. Nice chap, Godfrey. But narrowly-focussed. He got more than a bit stuffy about me opening this shop, felt I ought to have a crack at some academic posts, but teaching was never going to be my main aim in life. I'd had enough of it, the existence held bad memories for me, this was a release into a world that erected a sort of buffer against those outside. My aunt of revered memory provided the means by popping her clogs after remembering me in her will. I set up here. I don't make much of a living but I'm immersed, you know? Perhaps you might consider I'm hiding from my urges, or something, but who knows?'

'I'm no psychologist.'

'No. Just a copper. I wonder what your hidden desires are? You—'

'In your research into mediaeval Italy you spent some time at Chesters Fort.'

There was a slight pause before Proud replied. 'That's so...though the two weren't really connected, except in a small way. But I don't—'

'Did you carry out any catalogue work in the storeroom there?'

Proud folded his arms and glared at Grout. Suddenly, his eyes were harder. 'What's this all about? Why are you harassing me?'

'Harassing? You think this is harassment? I've hardly started yet,' Grout admitted calmly.

'I don't see why I should go over my past life for you.'

'I see no reason why I shouldn't swear out a warrant about the stuff you've got here.'

'It's not illegal!'

'But we could cause you trouble, looking just in case you were holding something...nasty.'

Proud held up his hands. 'All right, let's not get touchy. You want answers. Ask the questions.'

Grout smiled. 'Good. So I'll ask you again. Did you make a list of the items in the Chesters storeroom when you worked there?'

Proud shrugged. 'I did. But it was a while ago. I think I still have the list but I can't be sure. Let me think...' He moved around the room, soft-footed, twisting his lip. He stood before a tall cupboard, opened the door and stared at the piles of folders, binders, and dusty account books. 'A lot of this is stuff from when I took over. I've not dared touch it in case it all falls on my head. We need a woman's touch in this business. Fat chance, with my luck with women. But...I have a feeling, a vague recollection that I might have stuffed the list up here, on the top shelf.' He glanced over his shoulder at Grout. 'I suppose you would have imagined I kept whips and leather stuff and dildoes and all that here. Secreted away. But I'm a seller, not a practitioner. Just old files...' Dust floated down upon him as he reached up to rummage in the documents on the top shelf. He drew some down, inspected them, shook his head. 'Wrong. Not here. But...ah, of course!'

To one side of the cupboard was a wooden trunk of ancient vintage. 'My grandfather's when he went to university,' Proud explained. 'I remember now, all the stuff I had left when I have up at the university, I stuck it in here.'

'Your thesis?'

Proud shot a sharp glance in his direction. 'You'll have already heard I lost it in a fire.'

'Yes. How did that happen?'

'Long story.'

Grout sighed. 'That's what Professor Godfrey said. But he gave me a version.'

'I don't know whether he ever believed my story. But no matter, he'd seen my work, and he made out a case in my favour with the Senate. If it hadn't been for him, I wouldn't have been awarded my MA.'

'Not that you need it here.'

'You'd be surprised: it provides a veneer of respectability for some of my customers. Persuades them they're not really kinky, to think of their bookseller someone with a Masters degree.'

'Professor Godfrey said you claimed it was a bunch of students.'

Proud opened the trunk and began foraging inside its recesses. 'Something like that. Well, not exactly. You see, I was going out with this girl at the time. I spent the particular evening at her flat, a rather crummy place over at the West Road, and I got back in the early hours to find my place had been ransacked.'

'A burglary?'

Proud glanced at him, shrugged. 'Maybe. But I had a theory...You see, this girl I was dating, she'd been hitched up with this other guy for two years before she threw him over. He wasn't pleased, and when I got back to the flat and found the place had been turned over and my thesis destroyed, well, I thought of him straight away. My laptop had gone as well, so I thought if I went straight over to his place and confronted him maybe I'd get the laptop back at least. So I charged over there, two in the morning, hammered on his door, we had a right old barney but he denied everything...and there was no laptop. Anyway, I still suspected he had a hand in the business, but now, I'm not so sure...'

'The girl?'

'He married her a year later. C'est la vie. Hey, here we are. The very thing you're looking for, though God knows why! Voila! The storeroom list. I wonder why I ever bothered to keep it?'

Proud had drawn from the depths of the trunk a faded notebook which he flourished under Grout's nose. Grout took it from him and inspected a few pages.

'It appears to be full of scribbled notes.'

Proud stretched and yawned prodigiously, then scratched at his nose as though annoyed by dust arising from the trunk. 'Yeah, well, I think l you'll find what you seem to be looking for towards the back. The notes are some of the preparation stuff I did for my thesis: in the end that was about all that was left after the thesis and the laptop disappeared. There was some other stuff but after I got the MA award I threw it out. Don't know why I kept that notebook in fact. Overlooked it, I guess. Is that what you want?'

'May I take it away with me?'

'Hang it on your wall for all I care. It's yesterday's news as far as I'm concerned.' He eyed Grout for a moment then allowed a lascivious smile to touch his lips. 'There's far more interesting stuff in the back room, if you have that sort of inclination...'

With the notebook safely stowed in the glove compartment of his car Grout took the road to Beverley. He had little difficulty finding Paul Gilbert's house: it was large, rambling, standing on a corner where three lanes met and it commanded a pleasant view of the countryside around the village. Whether Gilbert made a good living from his photography Grout had no idea, but it was clear that the man lived in a certain style. The house was expensive, in a sought after area. The car wheels rasped over a gravelled drive as Grout drove up to the front door. The garage stood to one side of the house: its doors were open and the garage itself empty.

Grout parked, got out, went up to the front door and rang the ornately framed bell. He tried again but there was no reply. It seemed the house, as well as the garage, was unoccupied. Gilbert was not at home.

Grout waited, considering. He could go back to the office or he could wait here a while in case Gilbert turned up. He checked his watch and decided he would wait a little while, rather than return to York. He used his mobile to ring in to the office in York and left a message there for Cardinal, explaining he was waiting. He was told that the chief inspector had gone to Sheffield.

He sat on a bench in the front garden for an hour, enjoying the pale sunshine. He wondered what Cardinal was up to.

James Cardinal had been met at Sheffield railway station by a police car. He had decided to go there from Newcastle after receiving a phone call from the Sheffield CID.

The car took him swiftly away from the city centre and along the Glossop Road. It went past two sets of traffic lights, turned right, and slowed as it approached a street of houses that had been built perhaps eighty years earlier but which had now been turned into self-contained apartments, one up, one down. The gardens in front of the houses were in various states of disuse. There were already two police cars parked outside one of the houses, towards the end of a cul de sac. A small group of people stood to one side, rubbernecking. Cardinal got out of the car, ignored the throng and entered the house where a uniformed policeman was standing impassively on guard. As he entered the corridor leading to the downstairs flat he was met by an officer of the same rank as himself.

'Where is she?' Cardinal asked, dispensing with any ceremony.

The Sheffield officer directed him towards the bedroom.

She lay on her back, half on and half off the bed. Her arms were thrown back across the rumpled coverlet and her knees had buckled where she had slid downwards in the struggle. Death had not been kind to her: it had ripped away her beauty. Her hair had been torn out at one side of her head and the bar patch was stained with coagulated blood. The skin along her jaw line had been scratched as though a sharp instrument had scored its way across her skin, possible a ring. But it was the belt that had killed her. It was a cheap plastic belt, black in colour, shiny, an accessory Cardinal assumed might have been used on a woman's dress. But this belt had bitten cruelly into the woman's throat, effectively cutting off air to her lungs. As she had strangled to death her tongue had forced its way out between her teeth, and there was a trickle of blood on her left cheek where those teeth had clamped down in agony on her tongue.

'Who was she?' Cardinal asked.

The officer at his shoulder looked at him. 'My name's Carlton. Chief Inspector. You're Cardinal, I gather.'

When Cardinal glared at him Carlton raised his chin. 'Nice to know who one is talking to, no?' His voice was clipped, educated, no grace of a Yorkshire accent. 'Her name is...was...Eloise Parker, it seems. I'm told she was a photographic model, whatever that means, though it might well have been cover for a whole host of activities as we all know. There's some evidence she was legitimate, though how successful, one doesn't know.'

'Doesn't one?' Cardinal could not resist asking.

Carlton raised a dismissive eyebrow but did not rise to the bait. 'We've found a list of her contacts in the modelling world. It includes some reputable people. There's a scrapbook too, with some shots of her that were taken a few years ago, Not very much that's recent, so maybe she's been on the slide for a while, or maybe she's been concentrating on other activities. What exactly, I wouldn't know, but one can hazard a guess...But I was advised to call you...' There was an edge of hostility creeping into his tone. 'Call you, because she answers the description put out from Morpeth: they told me you'd be interested in this one. You can have it if you like. Never did like dealing with murder enquiries.'

Cardinal decided to capitulate to some extent: he was off his regular patch in any case. He took out a cigarette case, extracted a cigarette and offered one to Carlton. He rarely smoked these days, and even more rarely on duty, but there was a bitter taste in his mouth. He was hoping he could have questioned this girl. She would be able to tell him nothing about events at the George Hotel now.

"This girl...who checked into the George Hotel under an assumed name...I gather you found some connection with the dead man, Rigby.'

Carlton had refused the offer of a cigarette and was staring coldly at the one that remained unlit between Cardinal's fingers. 'This is a crime scene. I don't think it's a good idea if you smoke.'

'Of course. Sorry.'

'Yeah, we found a link. There's a bunch of letters in the bureau, unpaid bills, usual stuff...but there's one or two items which suggest he was paying the rent on this flat. We'll check, of course, but it looks like Rigby had set her up here. For obvious reasons, one would guess. All fairly recent, though.'

Cardinal took a deep breath. He nodded. 'And how long has she been dead?'

'The signs are it happened some time yesterday, but you know what forensic are like: they'll never give you a straight answer until they've gone through everything and thought it over. So, no precise time, but maybe early last night.' He hesitated, chewed at his lip. 'We do have a few other leads to follow up, even so.'

'Such as?'

The Sheffield CID man stroked his chin thoughtfully, and grimaced. 'Well, we know she was getting ready to go out somewhere when her visitor called. She had two appointments set up by a modelling agency but she had cancelled them, told them she'd be out of touch for a while. One of the staff at the agency told me early this afternoon that enquiries were being made about her and an address was given out, but for some reason no record was kept of the caller...it was done by phone. Slapdash, when you think about it. After all, how can the agency keep tabs and earn its money?'

'Anything else?' Cardinal asked.

'We've got the usual standby: a nosy neighbour. Surprising really, you'd think in flats like these people no longer have time to skulk behind curtains and watch what's going on. But the lady across the way...she's about seventy but still has her wits about her...she says there was a car parked in the street he for quite a while yesterday evening. Not a locally owned car: she knew all those, she reckoned. The vehicle was driven away about eight, returned again at ten for about an hour, and then went off again. She didn't see who was driving it. But she heard some odd noises in the street about midnight, she got up took a look outside and saw that the car was back. As far she could make out, anyway, because it was dark. And she wasn't really sure about the time.'

'Bit imprecise.'

'You said it.'

'Was it she who put out the alarm call?'

'Found the body, you mean? As a matter of fact, it was. No one else in the street seems to have noticed, but when she was up and about our neighbour saw the front door to the downstairs flat was ajar. She was on her way out herself, to visit the min-market down the road. Anyway, she nosed inside, called out to Miss Parker, and when she got no answer she took a look around.'

'Public spirited citizen.'

'Nosy old fanny, you mean. Still, she got the shock she deserved. Let out a scream, ran outside, back to her own house, rang 999. And that's when the cavalry arrived.'

'This old lady, she couldn't say what car it was she saw? Registration, that sort of thing.'

Carlton shook his head. 'You'd have thought not, wouldn't you? She couldn't give us a number, though she thinks it might have had a 6 in it...which is little help. But make of the car, that's another thing. She reckoned it was a Ford. How about that? You'd think an old girl like that wouldn't be interested in cars. But she regularly takes the Auto Trader apparently, even though she's not in the market to buy.'

'Misspent youth, perhaps?'

Carlton managed a smile. 'Back seat in inexpensive cars, you mean? Could be. But, there you are. I have to say, I don't take to the old girl much, but at least I can say we could do with eyes like hers among some of the coppers I have to work with.'

CHAPTER SIX

Grout was bored and frustrated. There had been no sign of his quarry. He felt he was wasting his time hanging around the house but Cardinal had been specific in his instructions and Grout knew better than to cross the old man. Not that he would get any Brownie points for hanging around: he'd get bawled out whichever decision he took. Cardinal didn't like to be kept waiting: he expected that matters would be followed through with expedition. Even if delay was due to no fault of Grout's.

He checked his watch, and decided he'd give it another half hour. In the event, it wasn't necessary. He caught a glimpse in his rear mirror of a car turning into the drive. He had pulled his own car forward half hidden behind a screen of trees so he knew the driver of the car coming up to the house would not see him immediately. He watched as the car nosed towards the garage. The driver killed the engine, got out of the car, locked the door and began to walk towards the house when he caught sight of Grout's vehicle.

He froze.

Grout had the feeling that the man was poised, contemplating flight: it would take little to send him irrationally leaping for his car. Then after a moment the man's shoulders slumped. Grout breathed a relieved sigh and got out of the car: he had no appetite for a wild chase in the countryside.

'Mr Gilbert?'

Paul Gilbert leaned back against the bonnet of his car and folded his arms as Grout walked towards him. Then, suddenly, the man folded forward, clutching his hands to his stomach. The sounds were unmistakeable: he retched, vomited in what seemed a panicked reaction. Grout hesitated, slowed, walked forward carefully.

'Are you all right?'

There was no reply apart from a continuation of the agonised retching. It finally ceased, dryly. Gilbert brought out a handkerchief and wiped his mouth and face. He stepped aside from the pool of vomit on the drive. He was sweating: Grout noted the perspiration glistening on his face.

'I'm sorry...I'm not feeling well.' Gilbert's voice was muffled by the handkerchief.

Grout thought it was quite understandable: even from where he stood some feet away from the man he had come to interview the stench of unassimilated whisky was palpable.

'We'd better go inside,' Grout suggested, extending a reluctant helping hand.

Gilbert ignored the assistance and lurched towards the front door of the house. He had some difficulty locating the appropriate key from the ring: Grout waited patiently then followed Gilbert into the house as he switched on the lights inside the entrance hall.

'I need a drink.'

Grout doubted that but made no demur: it was neither his house nor his stomach. They entered the sitting room. Gilbert staggered towards a drinks cabinet, poured himself a stiff scotch and then collapsed on the brocade settee without removing his coat. Grout looked around him.

It was an expensively furnished room with deep comfortable chairs, a piano, stereophonic recording equipment and a series of elegant photographs adorned the plainly papered walls. Several of the photographs were of elegantly posed girls, young, nubile, with the usual parted, expectant lips. He guessed they were examples of Gilbert's own work: the man did not seem to Grout to be the kind of individual who would be inclined to show the work of others.

Grout stared at the man sprawled on the settee, eyes closed, fingers loosely gripping the saviour whisky, intended to replace what he had already lost in the driveway. There was no doubt in Grout's mind he could easily haul Gilbert in right now, for being intoxicated in charge of a car. But there would be little point to that: it would be better to have a quiet chat with Gilbert in his own house, and see what transpired.

'You remember me, Mr Gilbert?'

It required a certain effort on the part of the eminent photographer to open his eyes: further effort led to his raising his head to blink, focus weakly, and then nod.

'You're that copper. You were at the George...I was questioned...what you doing here?'

'You've a good memory, Mr Gilbert, on even a short acquaintance. But regarding memory...was yours really that good, that day at the George?'

'What you talking about?' Gilbert said peevishly. He seemed in no mood to answer. His head dropped, he struggled to a more upright position and he began to retch again. The glass of whisky was spilled. Grout stepped back, looked about him, saw the half-open door across the room and wondered whether it was a bathroom. When he looked through the door he realised it was a small room that Gilbert had clearly furnished as a work room of sorts, for mounting and framing prints. It was cluttered with photographic material and equipment with some unmounted shots being some three or four feet across, but Grout suspected this was no Gilbert's main studio. That would be elsewhere, away from such clutter. But his attention was caught by one particular blow-up that occupied a position of prominence in the room.

90

It was the photograph of a girl, walking along a terrace beside a river

It took only moments for Grout to recognise the setting: the features of the woman were somewhat hazy, but the shot had been taken in the gardens of the George Hotel at Chollerford.

He stared at it thoughtfully for a little while, then turned and went back into the sitting room. Gilbert was sitting up, staring vacantly at the empty glass spilled on the rug in front of him. He seemed unhappy and depressed. Grout stood in front of him, waiting.

At last Gilbert looked up at him, eyes vacant.

'When you were questioned at the George Hotel, your answers seemed to me to be somewhat vague. But they interested me.'

'Is that so?' The words were belligerent, the tone defeated.

'They were somewhat precise.'

'What the hell you talking about? Isn't that a good thing?' Gilbert asked wearily. He stared unhappily at the stains on the rug before him.

'You answered with precision. Very, sort of, strict answers to questions. And you didn't exactly lie, did you? Perhaps...just left things out, is that right?'

Gilbert made no immediate reply, but there was a certain evasiveness in his glance. An edgy atmosphere seemed to be building up between the two men and it was sobering Gilbert quickly. Soon he would forget he was feeling ill.

'For instance,' Grout murmured almost casually, 'you said you didn't go in to her room with her. The inspector who questioned you, he put a certain interpretation on that...but another occurred to me. You might have meant you didn't go to the room with her: but that wouldn't preclude you from having visited her later on, would it?'

Gilbert opened his mouth as though about to reply, but then thought better of it and remained silent.

'And again,' Grout suggested, 'you said she gave you her name and that was all. Perhaps my ears are unduly sensitive but it seemed to me that there was a current of resentment in your tone when you made that statement. I wondered what that might be...so, what exactly did you mean in that statement, Mr Gilbert?'

Gilbert hesitated, then shook his head. 'I've nothing to add to what I said at the time. I don't know what you're trying to imply. I never stepped inside that room of hers. I never seduced her. I didn't really know her or anything about her. There was a bit of a chat, a drink, and then, after that, we went our separate ways. I haven't seen her, or heard from her since.'

'But you took her photograph.'

'Well, I...'

Gilbert seemed to be about to deny it but his glance flickered to the small room Grout had already inspected. He was suddenly very pale. Grout smiled at him but there was no warmth in the smile.

'When you were interviewed you specifically stated you had not taken any shots of the woman. But in fact you had. So why didn't you see fit to mention the photographs to the police? What were you trying to hide? Not just the photographs, I guess.'

'I wasn't asked about it,' Gilbert replied in a surly tone.

'Aw, come off it, Gilbert! I know you denied it! Besides, you knew we were trying to trace this girl. We had a description but that was all we had to go on. You must have realised that a photograph would have been invaluable to us. And you didn't even mention it? In fact, you denied taking any! Why? What were you trying to hide?"

'Hide? Nothing!' Gilbert licked dry lips, and he leaned forward, seizing his knees fiercely. He shook his head. 'Not telling you...I wasn't asked...I did nothing wrong!'

'You lied to us. You took a photograph of the girl; you knew we were looking for her; you withheld the photograph. This could lead to a degree of unpleasantness and harassment, Gilbert, believe me. Trouble could be heading your way.'

'No!' Gilbert's tone was strangled and he stared at grout in a desperation that was surprising. 'Look, I told you, I did nothing wrong! I wasn't withholding the shot deliberately, I mean, I had no intention of misleading anyone. But can't you understand? I didn't mention it because I just didn't want to get involved.'

'You'll have to explain that to me rather more fully,' Grout said coldly.

'I didn't want to get involved. All that police activity, the death at Chesters, I was shocked, I wasn't thinking straight. And the girl...'

'Yes?'

Gilbert heaved a sigh. 'All right, I chatted her up. I thought I was in with a chance, if you know what I mean. I tried to get off with her. And I got the impression she was leading me on. We walked on the terrace, I kissed her...and she agreed that I should go to her room after a short interval. But...' Gilbert looked at Grout with a sudden, sullen defiance. 'But when I went there, the bitch had locked the door. She had me standing there, almost pleading. And she stayed silent.'

'She was in the room?'

'I'm pretty certain of that. She was playing a game, wasn't she? Turning me on, then hanging me out to dry. And in the morning...she was gone.'

'You could have told us all this earlier.'

'What difference would it have made? I told you, I didn't want to be involved in all this mess. I didn't want to admit she'd made a fool of me...getting me interested, and then locking the bloody door!'

'And you're certain she was inside the room.'

Miserably, Gilbert shrugged. "I thought she was. At the time, I was certain she was. But now, thinking back, after I'd returned to my own room, and I was lying there frustrated I heard a car leave the George car park. Maybe she had already decided to leave the hotel; maybe that was her car. I don't know. The headlights flashed over my room ceiling. I remember thinking...'

He fell silent.

'It would have been better if you'd told us all this earlier. It could have made things easier for us. As it is, I think you'd better come with me to headquarters at York where you can make a statement—'

'Oh, there's no need for that,' boomed a voice from the doorway.

Cardinal smiled almost affably as he settled himself into a chair and stretched out his long legs. He sighed.

'That's better. Car seats do my back no good. I hope you don't mind, Mr Gilbert, my appearing unannounced like this. The front door was open. I saw my colleague's car. My name's Cardinal, by the way. Chief Inspector. You'd have expected Grout to introduce us. But there you are...'

Grout glared at the senior officer. Affability was a quality he had not come across in Cardinal before but there seemed to be a great deal of it in evidence now. It made him suspicious.

'I didn't realise—' he began but Cardinal waved him to silence with an expansive gesture.

'Don't worry about it, Grout, it's a general failing in the young and inexperienced. Social manners, I mean.

And I realise we were supposed to meet at headquarters, but I got tied up in other enquiries, couldn't have made it so when I got the message from you that you were still waiting to interview Mr Gilbert I thought I'd meet you here.'

He smiled at Gilbert.

'It's more cosy to have a routine chat here, isn't it, rather than at headquarters?'

Grout continued to stare at Cardinal, who had folded his arms, crossed his feet at the ankles and assumed the expression of a benign uncle.

'Now, Mr Gilbert, you were explaining something to young Grout here.'

After a brief hesitation Gilbert repeated what he had said to Grout, a little warily, but he seemed to relax somewhat as Cardinal frowned in understanding and nodded his head sagely.

'Well, I can see how you felt, and anyway, better late than never, hey? I mean, I know you have a reputation to maintain and as a photographer you wouldn't want to have your name dragged in with this unfortunate, and rather mysterious young woman, would you? But of course we'd like to have a copy of the photograph—'

'There's a big one in the room over there,' Grout snapped.

Cardinal eyed him as Gilbert babbled his assurance, rose and almost scurried into the other room. 'Yes, of course, you can take the print.' He seemed relieved by Cardinal's relaxed manner. Grout glowered, wondering what had brought about his senior's easiness: Chief Inspector Cardinal was normally renowned for his short temper and gracelessness with colleagues.

'How long have you been in the photography business?' Cardinal asked when Gilbert hurried back from the other room with the print in his hands.

'Twelve years, now.' Gilbert was sufficiently relieved even to indulge in a little boasting. 'In that time, I've made quite a reputation in certain circles—'

'And written a few books.'

'Well, they're really photographic essays,' Gilbert replied smugly. 'Shall I get some backing for this print or will you roll—'

'I suppose this line of work takes you about the country a fair bit,' Cardinal interrupted.

Gilbert shrugged. 'Certainly, around the northern counties. I've tended to restrict my work to Lancashire, Durham, Cumbria both for aesthetic reasons and as a way of staying away from some of those sharks down south. What they charge for gallery displays—'

'Very interesting.' Cardinal cut him short and turned to Grout. 'By the way, I've had another word on Clifford. He was seen in London yesterday afternoon, so he's not away yet. And we've also arranged to get details of the fencing arrangements in place for some of the art thefts last year. It would seem the pieces in question, which we are certain Clifford was involved with, were moved out to Switzerland to a receiver who was the director of a registered auction company in Basle. Each picture was catalogued then sold on to a member of the ring. Each 'sale' gave the picture provenance, a spurious legal coverage so that when it was passed on to a private buyer—not in open auction, of course—he'd have some paperwork to cover his back in due course. The buyers are probably up to the whole fiddle, up to their necks no doubt, but that's where we've got so far.'

Cardinal smiled. Grout stared at him, astonished that Cardinal would be speaking so freely in front of Paul Gilbert. Then Cardinal turned to the photographer. 'You've heard of Clifford, I suppose?'

Gilbert's features displayed only polite interest.

'Clifford? Is he a dealer?'

'I suppose you could call him that,' Cardinal said and laughed.

'I'm not sure...I can't really place the name among the people I've been dealing with over the years.'

'No matter. But these trips of yours, when you traipse around photographing things, I suppose you keep a record of them?'

'Naturally, since I have expenses to note for my accounts, and believe me I have a meticulous accountant. And I need the records for the shots, of course, to use them as the basis of captions I'll use later. You can forget so easily, when you're moving around. So I have records of dates, places, atmospheric conditions, lens focal number, exposure time, all the professional data that one needs to maintain to—'

'Yes, I'm sure. But it's just the places that I'm interested in.' Cardinal's tone was still affable and relaxed as he smiled benignly at Gilbert. 'So, let's test your memory. Let's take a random date. Let's say March 9 last year.'

'March 9.' Gilbert screwed up his eyes in thought. 'Not easy...March...hold on, yes, that's when I would be working the border castles. I was somewhere around Berwick round about that date. I was working my way gradually south.'

'Very good! So let's try another. February this year?'

'Beginning of the month, that's easy. I was in Leeds. After that I moved up to Durham but for details I'd have to consult my diary of course, my working diary that is—'

'Odd, really.' Some of the relaxed ease had disappeared from Cardinal's manner and there was an edge of steel in his tone. 'It's interesting, but on March 9 last year there happened to have been a theft of jewellery from the Delavere mansion in Northumberland. Not too far from Berwick, yes? And in February of this year an auction room in Sunderland was raided and some valuable silver stolen. You were in Durham, you say?'

'I don't see...' The immediate protestation on Gilbert's lips died. His eyes widened, and he stared at Cardinal as though he was looking at a particularly poisonous snake. 'You're hardly suggesting...Northumberland is a big county.'

'So is Durham,' Cardinal replied flatly. 'Equally, a job that takes you around the counties regularly can be good cover for nefarious activity such as the looting of auction rooms...or being on hand to accept stuff and dispose of it according to instructions.'

'You must be mad! You can't be suggesting—'

'I'm not suggesting anything yet, Mr Gilbert. I'm just asking questions. I'm simply pointing out a few facts to you. Now let's add to them. You stayed at the same hotel as a girl who was tied in with a member of a gang of thieves. You were seen with her, spoke to her, took her photograph—with or without her permission—tried to seduced her and then her boy friend got his skull crushed when you failed to get what you wanted!'

Gilbert bobbed up in his chair. Indignation scored his features, alarm squeaked in his voice.

'But what you're saying, it's all wrong! It's twisted! It wasn't like that! I was just—'

'You were just what?' Cardinal sneered. 'Just trying to make time with her behind her boy friend's back?'

'I tell you I didn't even know her, never met her before that night! I didn't know the man up at Chesters, and I didn't know he was linked to her! As for all this rubbish about thefts in the northern counties, I can't see what it's got to do with me!'

Cardinal silenced his tirade with a sharp gesture. He rose from his chair and advanced menacingly upon Gilbert. 'Don't play games with me, Gilbert," he snarled, injecting venom into his tone. 'You've already held up our investigations by withholding evidence.'

'I swear to you I never saw that woman before that night!'

'But you wanted to see her again, isn't that right?'

Gilbert's features were covered in a light sheen of sweat. He stared at Cardinal with the eyes of a dog that had been unjustly kicked.

'What car do you drive?' Cardinal asked quietly.

'It's...it's a Ford.'

'Colour?'

'Light green. What—'

'Is that the car at the garage?' Cardinal interrupted him.

'Yes, that's the one. Why do you ask?'

Cardinal grimaced, stared at him silently for several seconds then turned away and glanced at Grout.

'We found the girl.'

Grout made no reply. He was watching Gilbert. Plain terror now glared out of the man's eyes as he riveted his attention on Cardinal's back.

'I got a call from the Sheffield police' Cardinal said. 'They'd been presented with a corpse answering the description we put out. Her real name's Eloise Parker. So we won't need Gilbert's photograph of her now. She's been strangled. Not pretty any longer.' He looked at Gilbert, scowled. 'Maybe you'd like to take another photograph for your album. Before and after.'

'That's sick,' Gilbert croaked.

'Don't like 'em dead, do you?' Cardinal's mouth twisted unpleasantly. 'You been hitting the bottle hard tonight?'

Gilbert made no reply.

'Anyway, what were you doing yesterday and the day before? Working? Or checking on photographic agencies?'

'Why would I want to do that? '

'Because the girl worked as a model. My guess is you knew that...or guessed it.'

Gilbert shivered.

'I want to see my solicitor,' he whispered.

'That's your privilege,' Cardinal grunted, unmoved. Gilbert seemed incapable of movement, so he went on, 'Someone's been checking up on the dead girl...we know that from the agencies. A neighbour saw a car outside her place. Was it your car, Gilbert?' When Gilbert still made no reply, Cardinal suddenly snapped, 'Was it because she still wouldn't have you that you killed her?'

Gilbert leaped to his feet, stood there swaying unsteadily. He was shuddering and his eyes were wild. He glared at Cardinal, then at Grout and seemed to lose control. 'You're crazy! You can't believe that! I don't know what you're talking about! I was never—'

'A light green Ford was seen parked near the flat where the dead girl was found. It was your car, Gilbert—admit it! Come on, you've left a trail any fool can follow. First you withhold information, fail to help identify the girl, then you check with the agencies, find her address and go parking outside her flat! If it wasn't your fingers who throttled the life out of her—'

'This is madness! All right, I admit I went there, but I didn't...I never touched her! She was dead before ever I got into the flat.' He stopped suddenly, moaned. 'I want to phone my solicitor...'

Cardinal's tone was suddenly gentler. 'All right, my friend, you can talk to your solicitor. Use your own phone. But before you do, off the record, you might like to tell us your side of this story. What do you have to lose? If your story checks out we can let you just fade from the scene. No more hassle. So what do you say?'

Gilbert grabbed eagerly at the opportunity. The story was quickly, if incoherently, related. Grout listened while Gilbert gabbled his tale to Cardinal and recognised the bottled-up tension in the man, the sexual frustration, the blow to his pride by the rejection he had suffered at Chesters. Gilbert was a womaniser: there was no telling what degree of success he was accustomed to obtaining but it was certain that his failure with Eloise Parker had hit him hard. It had built up in a determination to seek her out, find her, persuade her into a closer relationship with him. What he had to say largely confirmed what Cardinal had already suggested.

It had not been too difficult, Gilbert explained, finding her. He had noted a certain grace, a way of carrying herself that had suggested to his experienced eye that she had worked as a professional model. He had his own shot of the girl so he had simply checked with the photographic agencies known to him, narrowed the search down to five firms and had been given access to their files in view of his own recognised status as a photographer. He had wheedled the information out of the last agency, learned her name and obtained her address, even though it seemed she had somewhat faded from the modelling scene of recent months. She lived in Sheffield. He had gone there.

'The flat was rented by Joseph Rigby,' Cardinal said coldly.

'I knew nothing about that.' Gilbert's immediate reaction changed and his eyes widened. 'Rigby...that was the man I found up at Chesters.'

'The same.'

'I didn't know that. I didn't know she was tied up with Rigby. How could I? I only met her for the first time at the George Hotel that night!'

'But how did you expect to press your suit,' Grout asked, 'by going around there?'

'Press his suit?' Cardinal asked, wonderingly. Grout was certainly of the old school, in spite of his age.

'I'd got her photograph,' Gilbert babbled. 'I just thought...if I went there and told them I'd kept it from the police, how I was looking after her, keeping her out of trouble, well, she might be...grateful, me helping her escape the attention of the police.'

'But not escaping your attentions,' Grout murmured. Cardinal was still staring at him, clearly amazed by Grout's choice of words. Gilbert rubbed his mouth with the back of his hand.

'So what happened when you got there?' Cardinal asked.

'I...I went to the address. She wasn't in. I parked, waited in the street for a few hours. I wanted to see her,' he said miserably. 'I must have been crazy. But after what happened...or really, didn't happen—at Chesters...At the hotel she was just another woman. But later...I couldn't forget her. It was like I was on fire. Couldn't keep still. Couldn't get her out of my mind.'

'So you waited in the street,' Cardinal said, prodding him on with his story.

'I left to get something to eat about eight: I hadn't eaten all day. Then I came back, waited, left to get some petrol before the station closed, came back and it was only then that I tried her door again. This time...it was unlocked. I went in. I called out.' He took a gulp of air. 'I called...and then I saw her.'

'What time was this?'

Gilbert shrugged, shook his head. 'I can't be certain. About twelve-thirty I guess. Maybe a bit later. I don't know. I was in shock.'

'Why didn't you report her death to the police?' Cardinal asked.

Gilbert hesitated. 'I was in shock. I got out of there fast, like a bat out of hell. But I did think of calling in. I took out my mobile phone, was about to make a report, then realised if I made the call it could be traced later even if I didn't leave my name...and I didn't want to be involved. Too many questions. Too much hassle. Too much explaining to do. So I never made the call. I kept my head down. I drove home.'

He shivered as though someone was walking over his grave.

'When I got home I couldn't sleep. I took a few drinks, but it didn't help I lay awake all night, absolutely terrified. I didn't feel I could go to the police, couldn't explain about her, about the photographs, finding her dead. I was afraid...'

'You've made things a damn sight worse for yourself,' Cardinal growled, 'and impeded our investigations. Couldn't you see delay would make your story more difficult to believe?'

'Look, I swear I didn't kill her! I didn't even touch her when I found her. I wanted her, I lusted after her, couldn't get her out of my mind. Now I can't get the memory of her' lying there, different, horrible...I can't eat. I can't sleep, I've been drinking, and when I got back here tonight and saw a strange car in the drive the panic just overwhelmed me. I've been sick as a dog...'

After Gilbert had been taken out to the car Cardinal joined Grout as he gathered up piles of photographs recently taken by the photographer on his expeditions. He watched sourly as Grout pushed a thick wad of prints on Chesters Fort into a file and tied it up with string.

'So, you reckon his story stands up?'

Grout tucked the file under his arm, looked down at the floor and shrugged.

'I don't know, sir. He's probably telling the truth, to my mind. What about your remarks regarding the Clifford gang? Do we have anything to back up the suggestion Gilbert was involved with Clifford?'

Cardinal grunted.

'Nothing. I was just testing the water, and trying to throw a scare into him.' He sighed. 'Well, we'll get a team in to turn this place upside down, see what we find. But like you I get the feeling Gilbert has no link to Clifford... and probably no link to Rigby. He just stumbled upon the body...'

'You're ruling out the possibility this could have been a crime—the killing of the girl—that had nothing to do with Gilbert getting revenge, or letting his anger overcome him when he got rejected a second time?'

'You think he's the type?' Cardinal didn't wait for an answer. 'No, I think Gilbert's no strong-arm man. I think we need to look elsewhere for the girl's killer.'

'Clifford?'

'He's still around in the background, isn't he?'

'So how do you see it all?' Grout asked carefully.

'I'm not sure yet.' Cardinal bit his lip, chewed at it thoughtfully. 'The evidence we've got so far makes a hazy picture but I think I can see some possibilities emerging. I have the feeling maybe Rigby was wanting to get out of the organisation, or possibly Clifford caught him with his fingers in the till on his own account, something along those lines. He didn't move fast enough and Clifford caught up with him. Clifford was either up at Chesters himself, or sent a contracted killer, and Rigby was sent to hell.'

'And the girl?' Grout asked.

Cardinal shrugged. 'She was probably tied in with Rigby. And knew too much for her own health. Clifford would have traced her easily enough. And now she's dead. He's tied up the loose ends, it seems.'

'That still doesn't explain what Rigby was doing up there at Chesters.'

Cardinal nodded. 'That's why I'd like to go through all the shots that Gilbert took in that area. I don't know what we'll be looking for, but who knows what'll turn up? Maybe he'll have photographed something that'll give us a lead. We know he went into the storeroom; he might have shot something that'll help us with the cataloguing...because I still have a gut feeling there was something in that storeroom that Rigby—and maybe Clifford too—wanted. We'll need to check his shots against the catalogue that young man Proud gave us.'

He led the way out of the house and stood in the driveway, sniffing at the air.

'First thing, we'll get a statement out of Gilbert. He'll be our guest for the night in the nick. By morning he might have cleared his mind a bit and come up with something else for us. Me, I'm off back to London. There's a conference with the Mets to attend. We'll be going over the cock-up that let Clifford dance free. The whisper is that he's probably already left the country. There are signs that his organisation is being wound up: the rats are scattering.'

He turned back to Grout.

'While I'm down south you get on with the footslogging. Check the photographs, check at Chesters again...you know the drill. We don't want to miss anything relevant. We need to know why Rigby was at Chesters. So concentrate on that. It will probably take time. The Roman Wall wasn't built in a day, you know.'

Grout was aware that Cardinal's classical allusions were few and far between, and usually inaccurate. There must have been something in his eyes that exposed his views to Cardinal.

The senior officer grinned contemptuously. 'Ah, hell. You know that stuff is all Greek to me!'

CHAPTER SEVEN

Grout spent most of the next morning working through Gilbert's statement, and checking the photographs that Gilbert had taken during his wanderings in Cumbria. In spite of himself he was impressed by the quality of the man's work but in a sense that made his task somewhat more difficult: the artistic arrangements and the effects of light and shade often did little to help identification of the actual sites, and he was forced to check through Gilbert's notes carefully, to ensure he could match up the photographs with the noted locations.

By the end of the morning he had set aside some forty prints which seemed to have come from the storeroom at Chesters and other areas in the close vicinity of the Roman fort. Armed with these, he set out once more for Chollerford. He stopped for lunch at Scotch Corner, then drove north up into the Cumbrian hills. It was a bright afternoon, with occasional clouds that darkened the fells with patches of shadow, and as he drove he caught occasional glimpses of buzzards circling on the upward spirals of warm air and sparrowhawks hovering at the roadside, searching for roadkill. He arrived at Chesters in the mid-afternoon.

The curator was helpful, even accommodating. It seemed he had been energised by the killing at the fort: the death of Rigby had caused an increase in visitors, all wanting to get a glimpse of the site where a man had lost his life in suspicious circumstances. The curator was more than pleased to offer what further assistance he could...the result might mean an even greater surge in popularity for visitors to the site.

'Who knows?' he said almost gleefully. 'You might even find another body?'

He was joking, of course, Grout concluded. One was enough to get on with. 'If you can just check these prints with me and note whether what we see in them is still in the storeroom, that could be of great help.'

The curator preceded him into the storeroom and together they checked the prints against the articles that remained in the storeroom. The curator identified some items as having been held in the main exhibition room upstairs; meticulously he then checked through the others as Grout ticked them off on the list he was compiling.

'You were here, I suppose, when Gilbert was doing this work?' Grout asked.

The curator wrinkled his brow. 'Some of the time. I had other things to attend to you understand, but I came down from time to time to check on what Mr Gilbert was up to. He took quite a long time, as I recall. He just didn't take shots at random. He moved some stuff so he could get a better angle or whatever. He had lights set up down here, of course, and was much concerned with the shadows that he arranged. And in that corner...'

Grout looked at him. The curator's lips were pursed in thought. 'I remember he was particularly fussed about that far corner. The lintel was a problem, and though he wanted to take a photograph of the item there in the end he gave up. He moved the piece, finally, and set it up over there, as I recall, and...'

His voice died away as uncertainty crept into his tone. 'Can I see that print again?'

'Which one?'

'The Mithraic head.'

'It's not one of the clearest shots he took. This one, you mean?'

'Yes, that's the one. Except...'

'What?'

'Well, he took this close-up of the Mithraic head, but there was something else, here you can see it in the photograph, that he used as a sort of background, so it's not very clear.'

'It's called an artistic arrangement,' Grout observed cynically. 'Not supposed to be in focus.'

'Yes, but you see the focus is too...wrong, to be able to make out the lettering on that military piece. It's half hidden by the head itself, and the lettering, all you can make out really is DI, and just there VE...'

'So?'

'Well, I don't know. It's a legionary piece, of course, of little importance for finds like these have been common along the Wall, but there's something about it I should remember, something that struck me at the time, when we moved it for Mr Gilbert's use...'

'I don't follow you,' Grout muttered.

No. That's right,' the curator murmured in a mystified tone. 'But as you see from this photograph it's quite a heavy piece. In some ways it's a typical item of statuary, some two feet high, thick-wristed, heavy-jowled, quite typical of the period. I remember thinking at the time, though, it should not really have been down here in the storeroom, it's in a decent condition, but I suppose it was down here because no one had got round to determining its provenance. At least, that's what I was thinking, but I was still puzzled. And now —'

'So where is it now?' Grout asked.

'Ah, well, that's it, isn't it? We moved it away from that lintel and over here for the photograph. And there's the Mithraic head that Mr Gilbert was using. But the other piece of statuary...'

'Is no longer here.'

'Can't understand that, can't understand that at all. It was heavy, you know. And who would want to take it? I mean, it's not an important piece, or it wouldn't have been down here, if you know what I mean. You see, the articles down here are of unproven worth, doubtful provenance...' The curator suddenly brightened. 'Ah, yes, that will be the solution. Doubt.'

Grout waited as the curator smiled in self-congratulation.

'You've lost me,' he said at last.

'Well, that's it, you see. The item was down here because it was of doubtful origin.'

'You mean it was fake.'

'Not, I'm not saying that. It was just that, probably, the piece had not been authenticated.' The curator shrugged. 'It's some years ago, and I can't quite recall... It wasn't worthy of display in the showroom and...wait a minute...there was a discussion of the piece, it was published, now where was that...?'

He picked absentmindedly at his lower lip with his fingers and made a little bubbling sound. Grout waited, staring fixedly at the photograph of the statuary. The legionary was half hidden by the piece of inscribed pottery and Gilbert had caught the sunlight lancing through the room and past the pottery. Dust hung in the air, minute spots of light: Gilbert had used the theme in the title he had written at the foot of the print, a suggested caption: Dust of Centuries.

The curator snapped his fingers. The sound echoed in the narrow room. He turned to Grout, a smile breaking out happily on his features, delight in solving a puzzle.

'Of course, of course, I recall it now. I read the piece some four years ago. It was discussed in a monograph, that was reprinted from a somewhat longer work. It was...let me think...but of course, it was Professor—'

'Godfrey,' Grout supplied and headed for the door.

'Professor Godfrey?'

The female secretary was perhaps forty years of age, slim, flat-bosomed and decidedly making no concessions to fashion behind her horn-rimmed glasses and determinedly plain blouse. She bore an air of overall efficiency that stamped her as a career woman—albeit against her secret wishes. She looked at Grout with cold eyes, as though inspecting a species of unimportant worm and the dissection of her glance was underlined by the stony edge to her tone.

'I'm afraid Professor Godfrey is unavailable.'

'Where can I contact him?'

The worm having been dissected was of little importance. The secretary turned back to the pile of papers on her desk. 'You can't.'

'Why not?'

The secretary now leaned forward, her nose like a predatory beak, ready to tear at her insistently annoying prey. In a supercilious tone she announced, 'The professor has gone south to collect some of his materials and make final arrangements for his trip.'

'Where's he going?'

She clearly felt it was none of his business, but rather than suffer his presence longer than was necessary she sighed and said, icily, 'Professor Godfrey is undertaking a short lecture tour of Germany and Holland. He speaks at The Hague next week. He has specifically informed me he desires no matters to be raised with him regarding work—'

'This isn't work.'

'—and he then intends taking a short holiday,' she stated, almost spitting out the words.

There was an odd undertone in her voice, as though she regretted that Godfrey had not seen fit to ask her to be a travelling companion. Secretaries often adored their bosses: perhaps this one fell into that category, one of hopeless, suppressed desire. The fact he had not taken her with him may well account for her bad temper now.

'Perhaps in the circumstances you can help me,' Grout suggested in an emollient tone.

'It's unlikely,' she suggested in an ungracious voice.

'He's an authority on antiques, is he not?'

The eyes behind the glasses glittered, at the thought that anyone should even ask such a ridiculous question of such an eminent man in his field.

'Of course he is,' she snapped. 'You must have seen him on television, even if you have never read any of his works.' She clearly felt reading of academic texts was beyond the capabilities of the inferior man standing in front of her. 'The TV people are after him at the moment, want to offer him a contract to do a series on his own collection of artefacts—it's unique, quite valuable, you know, built up over the years—but it demonstrates what kind of a man he is when he keeps them waiting while he takes a lecture tour, and then a holiday...Apart from which he does not want to show off his collection—he said it would almost be like committing adultery to allow the public to fawn over his favourite pieces.'

Her eyes had widened suddenly as the thought of adultery floated around at the back of her mind. Grout decided she was a very vulnerable woman, as far as Professor Godfrey was concerned. And he could hardly believe Godfrey would have made such a comment. His secretary probably read romantic novels in her spare time.

'Well, I suppose as an academic he needs the money from his lecture tour—'

'Professor Godfrey hardly concerns himself with such fees,' she snapped. 'He's quite well off, what with television, and his private collection. I sometimes think it must hardly be worth his while to continue at the university, but he is a man of principle and feels he has a duty...' She broke off suddenly, frowned, glared at Grout. Almost defensively, she added, 'He's been thinking of leaving, nevertheless. I'd go with him of course: he would need me.'

But you're not with him now, Grout thought to himself. He murmured, 'I'd really called to ask him if I could indeed borrow the book he had offered to lend me.'

'Book?' She was unconvinced, suspicious.

'Yes. He offered it to me when we met here on my last visit. He'd written a monograph about Chesters Fort, and Hadrian's Wall and a chapter of it was reprinted in book form. He said I could borrow it.'

She hesitated. 'He has a very good library.' She sniffed. 'But if he let everybody borrow from him—'

'It was his suggestion.' Grout smiled. 'He did offer to lend it to me.'

'He's not here to offer it now.'

Grout had suddenly suffered enough humiliation. He folded his arms and glowered at her.

'I came here to take up his offer. I intend to borrow it. I am staying here until you go fetch a copy. So fetch one. Now.'

He could see in her eyes the thought that perhaps she had made a mistake: he wasn't a worm at all.

He was an ill-mannered pig.

Grout took the monograph back to York with him. He stopped for a cup of coffee at a small cafe in Wetherby and glanced briefly through the text while he sipped at the hot drink. It was not a large work, with perhaps ten thousand words on the subject of Chesters Fort itself, and about another five thousands on the museum and the treasures it contained.

He soon founded the section that he wanted to check through. It was not particularly informative but it was all there was and it gave the reason for the relegation to the storeroom of the piece in which Grout was interested.

'The Wall itself has suffered the depredations of farmers over the centuries and it was only in comparatively recent times that the museum was able to identify and recover quite important items that had been scattered throughout Cumbria and Durham, and, occasionally, Northumberland. Among the many treasures however there are certain items of curiosity value. One piece comprises a legionary carving inscribed with the legend DIBUS VETERINIBUS. It was donated to the museum by way of a collection gathered by the Tapper family. It is interesting to note that the piece was at bone time used as a doorstep in the Tapper home: it was finally handed over to the museum in 1925.

There can be little doubt that the artefact is a manufactured one, in other words, it is not what it claims to be at first sight. The stone used is quite different from that normally used in statuary carved for use on the Wall. Also, I am confident that the piece dates from a period considerably later than its appearance and inscription would suggest. The cement used to repair a crack is of a different texture than that used in ancient times: sand and ox-blood did not possess such durability. So it must remain an interesting, if largely unimportant puzzle: why would anyone take the trouble to forge a piece of Hadrian Wall statuary when there was so much more freely available and of true historical interest in or near the fort at Chesters...'

Grout closed the book, sat back and thought for a while as he finished his coffee. His mind was still churning as he made his way back to his car. He agreed with Professor Godfrey: why go to the bother of forging a piece of statuary? Godfrey had regarded the piece as an uninteresting curiosity, but Grout wondered just how secure was Godfrey's opinion?

The opinion was perhaps brought into question by the fact it seemed someone had taken a considerable amount of trouble to remove the statuary from the museum...when Rigby was killed in the vicinity. Were the two facts really linked?

It could be that there was a connection: if so, Grout was unable to see what it might be.

He returned to headquarters in a thoughtful mood. He stared at the prints he had obtained from Gilbert and re-read Godfrey's account of the museum and its holdings. There was something wrong, he felt it in his bones, but he was unable to put a finger on what was bothering him. He turned to Philip Proud's notebook and read the catalogued list in the back. The legionary piece was not mentioned. Maybe it hadn't been there when Proud made his notes—in which case it had been placed in the storeroom relatively recently. Or was it that Proud hadn't notices, or thought it unworthy of attention?

Grout's head was buzzing. He felt he was getting nowhere, and he began to doubt the wisdom of trying to follow a lead that probably took him nowhere. He flipped over to the front of Proud's book, to read the notes he had made on his thesis. Most of it was gibberish to Grout, and of course it had nothing to do with legionary statuary. The account in Proud's thesis was postulated on events in Italy, not Northumberland.

He felt depressed. There was nothing to go on. He was wasting his time. He had hoped the day would give him something to present to Cardinal: he could visualise the glowering look he'd get from the Chief

Inspector when he reported what was effectively failure.

The thought made him bad-tempered. When the telephone rang he grabbed at the receiver and snarled his number into it.

'My, my,' came a light and cheerful voice. 'Wrong side of the bed, Grout? Or the wrong bed?'

'Proud,' Grout said grumpily, recognising the voice and the inanity of the man's humour.

'The very same. I been trying to contact you.'

'And now you've done so. I suppose you want your notebook back.'

'Hell's flames, stuff the bloody thing into the dustbin if you like! No, there's something else I wanted to mention to you. Funny, really. It's something I been puzzling about for a couple of days.'

'Tell me,' Grout said, hoping he wouldn't.

'The photograph,' Proud said. 'The one they published in the newspapers. You know, location of where that man Rigby got knocked off.' There was a pause. 'Well, not just the location, but that mug shot of the deceased. The two together...it reminded me eventually, the link...you see, I think I recognised this guy Rigby. Shoved it to the back of my mind, but hey, out it popped again! Like some of the old fellers who come into my shop. Won't be denied.'

'What are you talking about?' Grout asked wearily.

'I told you. I remember seeing him before.'

'Get to the point,' Grout said. 'I've had a frustrating day.'

'Frustration...it's the main underpinning of my business, I reckon. However...thing is, I remember now. That guy Rigby. I saw his mugshot in the paper, but I seen him before. Maybe three months ago. In the shop.'

116

'Three months ago? And you remember him?' There was doubt in Grout's tone, but something warm growing in his chest. 'Tell me.'

'He came to the shop. Had a chat with me. Came to see me specially.'

'Specially?'

'Told me he was a publisher's rep. But it was my work he wanted to talk about. That's why I remember him.'

Grout took a deep breath. 'I think you'd better tell me all about it.'

CHAPTER EIGHT

Philip Proud sat in his easy chair, cocked one leg over the arm, raised his whisky in a cheerful gesture and smiled.

'Sure you won't have one?"

'This is a duty call, not a social occasion,' Grout growled.

'Get on, you ought to take one with me. Who's to know, except you and me? Fact is I'm celebrating: I bought three hundred copies of Cindy and the Whipmaster last week—thirteen quid a time—and the news came through that the Metropolitan Police have seized copies as obscene. Result? I'm sold out at forty quid a time. So have a drink! We deserve it.'

'You don't exactly deal with art then,' Grout commented sourly.

'Commerce is the game! Give the market what it wants!' Proud sipped his whisky, smoothed his moustache with a satisfied finger, and gave Grout a dazzling smile. 'Life can be good,' he purred.

'Until you get raided.'

'Hey, the copies have gone!'

'Anyway, I'm not interested in the porn industry. I came to talk to you about Rigby.'

'So you did, so you did.' Proud nodded, put down his glass on the coffee table beside him. 'Funny that: I should have rumbled him at the time, straightaway I mean, but I suppose I was flattered and then nothing came of it and I just sort of forgot what had happened.'

'Tell me exactly...what did happen?'

'Well, it was like this...I got a phone call, he called himself Barnes, and he said he worked for a publishing firm. He explained he'd heard about my thesis and thought there might be a chance his company would be interested in publishing the completed work.'

'So he came to see you?'

'That's right. And I didn't sort of twig that the approach was a bit unusual. I mean, normally, you have to struggle to get yourself into print, if you know what I mean. And here was this guy talking about publishing a text on an obscure subject...but I guess I wasn't really thinking straight at the time.'

'And this man Barnes—'

'It was Rigby. I know that now. Like I said he came to see me, we talked about the thesis, discussed its publication, and he wanted to take the thesis away with him for closer inspection. Give it to a reader, he said, an expert in the field. Of course I told him I couldn't do that since it was still at a draft stage, the material was raw, needed polishing before publication and I needed to check it through before it was submitted to the senate. After that...'

'He didn't suggest you ran a copy off for him, from your computer?'

Proud shrugged. 'He did, but I couldn't allow that. I mean there's guys out there who plagiarise your work...'

'Even an obscure thesis?'

Proud bridled a little. 'Hey, I'd slaved over that stuff! Though it all seems so long ago now, a different world experience like, if you know what I mean...Anyway, though he seemed disappointed he didn't make a song and dance about it. Instead, he said they'd like to consider it when it was finally ready but meanwhile it'd be useful if he could read through it, give it a sort of initial going-over. I could see no reason why not so I agreed, and I found him a chair where he could settle down and read it, browse through it. In the end he didn't take as long as I thought he might. In fact he seemed to concentrate on one particular section, rather than plough through the lot. Took him about half an hour, that's all, and he made some notes, but I was glad to see the back of him really because I had a hot date and I wanted him out of there. So he pushed off at last, after saying he'd be in touch again after he'd talked things through with his managing editor. He never did come back, though; I can't say I was surprised. There was something odd about the whole thing, I thought at the time. Nothing I could put a finger on, of course, and in any case it didn't loom large in my mind the way life was going just then...'

The girl, Grout surmised. 'How long after that did the thesis get lost?'

'Couple of weeks, I suppose.'

'You didn't link the two events in your mind? The visit from this man Barnes, or Rigby as he really was, and the destruction of the thesis?'

Proud wrinkled his nose and scowled. 'No. Why should I? I mean, if he really wanted to publish the book he could have waited, it would be just a matter of weeks, and then I was pretty sure at the time how it all came about. I thought I knew who'd stolen the laptop and destroyed the thesis, and why...but are you now saying there was a link? That it was Rigby who broke into my flat and did the damage?'

'It's a possibility.'

'But why should he do that?'

'Why did he want to read the thesis in the first instance?' Grout countered. 'For that matter, how did the thesis even come to the attention of a man like him in the first place?'

Proud was somewhat nettled for a moment, as though Grout was denigrating the value of the work he had been undertaking for his thesis. 'Hey, you know I did get a spot on television, you know! I was interviewed as one of Professor Godfrey's students and I did mention my work then. I remember, the TV crew had come on site and talked to me...it wasn't tied in with the Prof's show...and I remember thinking he was a bit cool about it all. He even suggested I shouldn't have discussed matters of academic importance like that on the box. Huh! It was all right for him to prance about on his own programme, but he was clearly miffed that I'd got a bit of limelight on me. Still, I shouldn't complain, should I? I mean, he came through for me later, after the thesis was destroyed.'

'I suppose Rigby could have seen you on the box,' Grout murmured doubtfully. 'Anyway, you say he'd concentrated on just one section of the work when he was with you, reading it.'

'That's the way it was.'

'And the section?'

There was as short silence As Philip Proud concentrated. Then his brow cleared. 'Yeah, that's right. A sort of minor section in the whole work, really. Not really important, not essential to the main themes. A bit of romantic stuff I'd put in for colour...you know, stop the academics who'd be reading the thesis from yawning too much. That's right. The section on the Sforzas. That's it...the Paduan Conspiracy.'

Proud got up, poured himself another drink, caught Grout's glance and raised an eyebrow. 'Change your mind?'

Grout shook his head. 'The Paduan Conspiracy.'

Proud settled back in his chair. 'Long time ago, and I've kept no notes.'

'Do your best,' Grout said ironically.

'I won't be able to vouch for the accuracy of the dates.'

'Facts will do. I'm not interested in dates. Just tell me what you remember about that section in your thesis.'

Proud nodded, wrinkled his brow. 'Yeah, well, I suppose most of it is still floating around inside my head, in spite of the porn I've been reading recently. And in a way it was all about porn, though of a different kind. Power, wealth, the pursuit of these can be kind of pornographic, can't it? Right...Lodovico Sforza, member of a powerful, rich and corrupt family in mediacval Italy. Like the Borgias, the Sforzas have left their mark on history. A bloody mark.'

He lapsed into thought, smiling slightly. Grout waited.

'Yeah, he was a powerful man, was our Lodovico. Patron of the arts, of course, like they all were, those mediaeval dukes in the city states, but corrupt too, and murderous. Lodovico himself, well he became regent of Milan while his nephew the Duke was under age and then it seems the nephew died in rather mysterious circumstances, at which point Lodovico jumped into the vacant dukedom like a shot. Was he involved in the death of his nephew? Hey, this was mediaeval Italy!'

He sipped his drink, nodded enthusiastically. 'Anyway, there's the nephew dead, Lodovico is Duke of Milan but he needs support and he runs around trying to get the support of France, and then, when the French king decided he'd like to have Milan for himself, Lodovico turned to the Holy Roman Emperor, Maximilian , but by then he's got plenty of enemies and he is destined not to last long as Duke. He died in prison eventually, captured by the French, rotting away in the dark. Sic transit gloria...'

Patiently, Grout reminded him, 'The Paduan Conspiracy.'

'Yeah I was coming around to that. There were several attempts on his life of course: it sort of went with the job. But one of them occurred when he was visiting Padua to drum up support for his dukedom. He was away from his power base; it must have seemed a good opportunity for his enemies to strike at him. Yeah, the conspiracy, the plotting in Padua...As I recall, there were five of them: oddly enough, I can even remember their names. Bocanegra, Cardenas, Perez, Boldini, de Rivera. Funny, that. But those were the guys.'

'They don't sound particularly Italian.'

'Hey, even the Borgia family weren't Italian: they came from Xativa, in Spain. But like you say, these guys weren't all Italian. Three of them were Spanish exiles. Boldini himself, he wasn't even a gentleman, it seems, though he was more than handy with a knife.'

Proud paused, screwed up his eyes, stroked his moustache in a preening, self-satisfied gesture. 'Yeah, that was it...Lodovico Sforza visited Padua in the December of that year...what bloody year was it, I don't recall, dammit... Anyway, it was the year when his daughter was married into the Scorzi family, so it's easily checked if you think it's important. He had intended staying for the wedding but then moving on, but bad weather delayed him, stopped him travelling on. It gave the conspirators a few more days to plan their project.'

'Project?'

'Assassination.' His face lit up. 'That's it, I remember now, it was the fifteenth of December, a festive occasion, a grand get-together in the Hall of Princes. A meeting that was to be the prelude to a bloodbath.'

'The conspirators—'

'Don't rush me! I got to go through this slowly. As I recall it was the inquisitors employed by Sforza who squeezed out most of the details from Perez later, they paid a lot of attention to his genitals as I recall, before he told them what they wanted to know. They garrotted him shortly after, when they were convinced there was nothing more to be got out of him. As for the story he told them...it seems Perez had bribed two sentries to manage an entry for himself and the other four murderers through the north gate. They gained access to the ducal wing; they concealed themselves in the antechamber to Sforza's private rooms.' He grinned suddenly. 'Ah, yes, and there was Carlotta. You know, I'm surprised Hollywood never got to make this story into film. Carlotta Fantini. A lady of Padua...a lady of some repute, if you know what I mean...'

Grout waited as Proud seemed to lose himself in thought, probably erotic.

'Yes, good in bed, by all accounts. It seems that Sforza had made an assignation with the lady in question for entirely understandable reasons. He had been happily married, you know, though that didn't stop him having two regular mistresses. But he was away from home...and had his wife died by then? I rather think she had. Anyway, he was a virile guy and needed distraction, it seems.'

Proud nodded to himself, almost approvingly. 'Sforza now, he was a man of precise habits. The meeting he had arranged with the courtesan was to be at 1.15 in the morning apparently—after he had dealt with affairs of state—and Carlotta turned up at 1.12 precisely. She entered the anteroom and was seized by the conspirators, threatened with a knife, while Sforza was still preparing himself in the bedroom for a night of frenzied activity. He was reputed to be a man of prodigious appetites, sexually..."

Proud sipped at his drink, waved the glass theatrically.

'His loins must have been itching, one imagines, and his temper fraying when she had not entered the room at 1.20, so he opened the doors to find out what had happened to her. You can imagine him bawling out, demanding where the hell she had got to, can't you?'

Grout raised an eyebrow but made no comment.

'Anyway, as he entered the anteroom he was faced by the five conspirators. You know, Sergeant, you have to admire Sforza: a man of courage and determination as well as sexual prowess. Or maybe he was just enraged at having his little tete-a-tete disturbed. Anyway, in the next few minutes he got through that room with only a couple of wounds to his arm and hand. Maybe the five conspirators were incompetent; maybe Sforza's bulk intimidated them; maybe Carlotta herself impeded them in their attempt to stab the man they hated. However, with Carlotta screaming, yelling, squirming, Sforza bellowing curses, fighting like the madman he was—reputedly—he got through that throng and was quickly assisted by his personal guards who burst in upon the struggle.'

'The conspirators were captured?'

'Cut down. Perez was wounded and taken into custody. He was racked, tortured to confession. Two others were despatched there and then, I believe. Another died by the hand of the Duke of Milan himself. One man, however, managed to make his escape in the confusion. Boldini. Seems he had the sense to retire early from the fray and make himself scarce.'

'What happened to him?' Grout asked.

Proud shrugged.

'That's where the questions start. The event was naturally a scandal, and much talked about, particularly when the confession of Perez was noised abroad. But Boldini...well, nothing more seems to have been written about him. The Vatican eventually published some archival papers in 1962, but they received little attention at the time. I dug them up when I was doing my research but they told me little...and really it was all a side issue to my work if you know what I mean. Sort of romantic, but not essential. Still among the papers was a report from a certain Robert Buckingham who at that time had attended the court in England. He had, it seemed, been in the pay of Sforza. The usual Janus-headed spy, informing on both sides, Milan and England. According to his account Boldini managed to get out of Italy, and made his way to England. Buckingham's account was precise and confident, which would suggest he himself might have had a hand in the escape.'

Proud smiled, caressed his moustache.

'Interesting fellow, really, the Boldini guy. He was a stonemason by trade, it seems. Not your usual kind of gentlemanly murderer. But he was certainly a man who was able to grab at his chances when they arose. He managed to get out of Sforza's chambers and escape the mayhem—where Carlotta herself got knifed, a superficial wound it seems—by diving through the window. But not before he managed to dive through the window onto the tiles roof below he also managed to sweep up from Sforza's night table several items of jewellery where Sforza, presumably to impress or pay the lady Carlotta, had displayed them. Whatever, he got away, bodily and in possession of a haul. By all accounts it included some of the collection of the Abbé Casalucci.'

'I'm afraid that rings no bells for me,' Grout admitted after a short silence.

'Your historical knowledge must be on a par with your pornographic leanings,' Proud said in regret; shaking his head. "Sadly deficient...your early education must have been misdirected. But you never went to public school, I imagine. So, I suppose you've never heard of, or seen, Carnetti's Madonna of the Seven Wells?'

'You're right. On all counts. I haven't. So what?'

'An interesting painting. Not least because on the left breast of the Madonna there appears to be pinned a jewel. It has some religious significance though quite what escapes me for the moment. However, the jewel is priceless, and was said to be the worth of the ransom of seven kings. To us, I suppose we'd say it was of incalculable value.'

Grout frowned. 'Your tenses are confusing. A painted jewel. Was it just a painting, or did it exist?'

'It existed. It was pinched by Boldini.'

'You mean it was part of the haul he grabbed making his escape?'

'Precisely. Some of the Casalucci jewels turned up later...I imagine Boldini was forced to sell them cheaply to pay the necessary bribes to get out of Italy and disappear.'

'And?'

Proud shrugged.

'You tell me. We know he fled that night with the jewel. We know from Buckingham's account that he came to England. Sforza's assassins followed him no doubt, once Buckingham reported to them. They wanted revenge—and, presumably, what was left of the jewels. But the trail went cold from there. A long silence, one might say.'

'So the jewels were never recovered?'

Proud shook his head. "No, no, some of them turned up later like I said. As for the rest well, the only jewel that was ever identified as important was the Madonna jewel. It was never recovered. On the other hand, while I was doing my research and being sidetracked by this murderous tale I did come across a piece of in information which seemed, shall we say, irrelevant? It was noted among the Vatican papers, a sort of side note if you will, that a man called Bollands died at Alnwick, some fifteen years after the Paduan Conspiracy.'

'In the Vatican papers?'

'Correct.'

'Alnwick is a hell of a way from Italy. I don't follow—'

'Neither do I, really, not entirely.' Proud finished his drink. 'But it's interesting, isn't it? I took a look at parish records. This Bolland, mentioned by the Vatican, turns out to have suffered a violent end. Murdered in Alnwick. I told you that Boldini had been a stonemason by trade. The son of the murdered Bolland was also a stonemason: he worked on the castle at Alnwick. And when he was buried in his turn there was some sort of fuss with the bishop. It ended with the removal of Simon's tombstone. It seemed the stone carried some kind of offensive inscription.'

'Did you find out what the inscription said?'

'Can't remember exactly now but it was something like To the ancient Gods of Rome...that sort of thing.'

Grout grimaced.

'I can understand the bishop wanting that removed from the churchyard. Even so, I fail to see what you're getting at.'

Proud shrugged cheerfully.

'Nothing specific, really. Just retailing some interesting facts. You're the detective: up to you to try to string them together into something meaningful. But they were all in the section I did in the thesis...the section Rigby was so interested in. And, well, I did my own bit of theorising, too, I guess.'

'Tell me.'

'Well, look at it like this. Boldini stole the jewel of the Madonna and somehow got out of Italy. Sforza used his intelligence services and discovered from his English informant Buckingham that Boldini had entered England. Sforza sent men after him. Thereafter...silence.'

Proud screwed up his eyes in thought, squinted at Grout.

'But it seems that about fifteen years later, something crops up in the Sforza papers: there's a mention of the man called Bollands being murdered at Alnwick, in Northumberland. The papers eventually found their way into the Vatican library, where I finally came across them. This raises a number of questions, as far as I can see.'

'Such as?'

Proud flicked up a finger. 'First of all, why should Sforza record the death of an obscure stranger in Northumberland? Answer: in all probability the man was not a stranger.'

'You're suggesting Bollands and Boldini are one and the same.'

'The theory is not all that wild,' Proud insisted. 'Look at the facts and remember that Simon Bollands, buried in Alnwick, was a stonemason. Isn't it reasonable to suppose he followed in his father's trade? And Boldini had been a stonemason before he started hiring himself out as an assassin.'

'Yes, but—'

'No but about it, Sergeant. Facts is facts, if you'll excuse my ungrammatical construction. But then there's the second question in my mind.' He flicked up a second finger. 'What happened to the jewel of the Madonna? It seems to have disappeared, not heard of again.'

'Not accounted for?'

Proud shook his head vigorously.

'Never. It's quite certain Lodovico Sforza never recovered it. But it looks as though he was hunting for it, as well as revenge, when Boldini was struck down. So what happened to the jewel?'

He grinned at Grout.

'Which brings me to the last question. It hadn't occurred to me that I should link the two questions until today—'

'The Paduan Conspiracy and Rigby?'

'That's right. But after talking to you a sort of link popped up in my mind. You have to wonder why a man like Rigby would be interested in my thesis, and in particular the section on the Paduan Conspiracy.'

'So theorize to me.'

'Hell, no,' Proud shook his head, waved his arm in the general direction of the bookshop downstairs. 'I've got enough on my dirty little mind not to want to get involved in real crimes. It's up to you, the copper, to root around in these old histories to see if they're relevant. But why did Rigby come to see me? What did he hope to gain from reading my thesis?'

Grout was silent for a little while, staring at the young bookseller. Then he rose to his feet.

'I can guess,' he said.

Grout returned to headquarters in a thoughtful mood. He was rather disappointed that Cardinal was not there and was even more disappointed to learn that he could not be contacted. Grout waited for an hour or more then wandered out into the city for a meal.

He ate alone in a small restaurant in the city centre. The menu was Italian, and his thoughts wandered over what Proud had told him. Later, he walked towards the cathedral precincts and wandered through the close, stared down at the foundations of the great building where they had been strengthened to prevent an otherwise inevitable collapse. The building had lasted for hundreds of years: so had the Sforza papers, buried in the archives of the Vatican.

Grout did not feel he was an imaginative man, though Cardinal gave him credit for being so. There were occasions when he was fired with excitement by mundane things: sometimes a law case he was reading would enthuse him by virtue of the abstruse point of law raised. And he felt a vague excitement now, not so much at the thought of discovering who had killed Rigby, and why he had been murdered, as by the realisation that the dead man would seem to have unlocked a secret that had lain hidden for five hundred years. For Grout was quite certain of it: he could not yet prove it, but he was convinced that Rigby had been after the jewel of the Madonna.

He would have liked to discuss it with Cardinal. He didn't have the chance. Cardinal woke him early next morning, the phone ringing insistently at Grout's bedside. Cardinal's tone was sharp, his instructions precise.

'Shift your arse down to London this afternoon. And bring your passport. That bloody man Clifford, he's skipped. He left the country last night.'

CHAPTER NINE

For the proletarian and the hungry there was boiled beef and horseradish sauce, venison or boar. For those with cultivated palates there was shish-kebab served on flaming swords, or schnitzel. There were mock chickens available—boneless pastry carcases filled with ersatz chicken meat side by side with splendidly layered chocolate cakes. There were vegan options. Lobsters were being served for the vegetarians, lifelike but constructed from soya beans. The air was fragrant with the scent of flowers and food: the restaurant bustled with custom and conversations fluttered half-heard through the echoing room.

'Interpol expense accounts must be lavish,' Cardinal remarked with a hint of displeasure in his tone.

The man called Enders laughed. 'If you think this is lavish, go to one of the restaurants used by our members of the European Parliament. I don't eat here every day, I should advise you, but this is an occasion when I must honour the visit of English colleagues. I think it is of importance that I show you the best. Even the sandwiches provided here, you should try them. They are concoctions of fire and spice and dynamite, caviar and pfefferoni.'

'I'll try them by way of celebration when we get our hands on Clifford,' Cardinal growled.

Enders nodded. 'You tell me it is murder as well as the theft of ancient artefacts that he is now wanted for.'

'It looks that way. When she skipped the country I feared we'd lose him in Europe—there are so many opportunities for a man of his kind to vanish under cover of a new identity. But with the co-operation and assistance of Interpol—'

'It's what we exist for,' Enders murmured, 'and we can also enlist the Italian Art Squad in the matter of the tracing of antiques. They have been very active of recent years, not least over the matter of the tombaroli, the men who dig in ancient Etruscan tombs and sell what they find to museums and art galleries, assisted one is forced to admit, by seemingly respectable art dealers and auction houses. As for Interpol, as you know we have no police powers but as an information agency we can help in the tracking down of criminals, not least those involved in this international conspiracy of theft—antiques from Florence and Rome, Baghdad and Istanbul, lootings from Afghanistan and Iran—it is a wide ranging business, I assure you!'

He pushed aside his plate and leaned forward, a plump-featured man with a hairless head. His eyes were like little black buttons, sharp, bright.

'I have put on alert my contacts in the German and Austrian police and have been promised full co-operation. It would seem your man Clifford has been a little careless in his haste to leave your jurisdiction: he has used a false passport which was already on our files. With a degree of luck we may well be able to place our hands on him by tomorrow evening.'

'I confess to being a little surprised by your speed of reaction,' Cardinal admitted. 'I hardly thought you'd pick up his trail so quickly.'

Enders shrugged and gestured to the hovering waiter for coffee. The light from the ornate chandeliers in the ceiling glistened on his hairless skull.

'Chance played its part,' he murmured, almost apologetically. 'As you know, the organisations that have linked together to form a ring, dealing with unprovenanced art works, have been successful for some years. This was partly because Switzerland and Germany lacked specialists dealing with such matters; partly because we had no over-arching organisation that could co-ordinate our individual systems; and not least because we were facing large, reputable museums who were reluctant to admit either that they had been indulging in such trade nor to confess to holdings that were of suspect provenance. The museums live in a competitive, secret world of their own, and there are many curators who seek only the glory of their collections, without worrying too much about where the artefacts may have been looted—to the despair and fury of the archaeological world.'

He paused as the coffee was served.

'Still, there was considerable impetus gained when the Italians decided to set up their Art Squad under the direction of Senora Carmela Cacciatore...indeed, I believe that the squad has recently been reinforced by a compatriot of yours, a Mr Arnold Landon.'

'Our paths haven't crossed,' Cardinal admitted.

'Of recent months we have managed to assist the Art Squad in tracing some five hundred valuable antiques and paintings in Switzerland, Germany, Canada and the United States. Two successful prosecutions have been brought in Italy against individuals who played a leading role in this international art conspiracy, we've built up a blacklist of agents handling such works and we are currently co-operating in the investigation of individuals we believe have been involved in the handling of items from the looted Baghdad Museum and the thefts arising during the Libyan uprising.'

'I heard you'd made a number of arrests.'

'That is so. One in particular will be of interest to you. He is an individual called Severini, on whom we found a considerable number of incriminating documents which told us he had been dealing extensively with agents in England. He is not particularly interested in spending a long time in prison, and a little persuasion, some direct threats, and the prospect of a long period within stone walls have led him to co-operate: he admitted finally that much of his dealings have been with a man called Clifford, in London.'

Enders added cream to his coffee and watched it swirl, thick and white on the black surface.

'This is why we were able to put a trace on Clifford almost immediately. In a sense he was already in our purview. We were expecting to advise Scotland Yard to bring him in within the next few weeks, and then when it came to our attention that there was an operation being directed against him we put some muscle into our side of things. It took us only three hours to learn that after he left London he surfaced in Berlin under an assumed name. We contacted the German police, a series of raids were carried out upon known receivers and that brought a welcome haul of items and information.'

'But no Clifford.'

'Sadly, no. He had already moved on.'

'But you know his destination?'

Enders nodded. 'We believe he is located near the Bodensee.' He sighed. 'This Clifford, he is an old adversary of yours I believe. A slippery customer, as I think you would describe him in English. The Bodensee is a natural place for him. It puts him one step ahead of the forces of law. On the Bodensee there are many passenger and freight boats coming in all the time, from Switzerland, Austria and Germany. The traffic is international. We have open borders, of course, unlike the situation fifty years ago and if Clifford is put to flight it is not difficult for him to escape in various directions.'

'But you think he is here, on the Bodensee?'

'Do not be so anxious, my friend. He is not running at the moment. Something would seem to be holding him here.' Enders smiled and finished his coffee. 'He is here, we are sure of it. He is accompanied by four others; they have rented a villa overlooking the lake. There is the possibility that preparations are currently being made for a swift disappearance but there is also the chance that some kind of coup is being planned.'

'Is that why the polizei haven't gone in on them yet?'

'Something like that. First, there is some kind of dispute over paperwork: you know how bureaucrats can delay things, warrants, search documents, that kind of thing. And if it involves extradition there are other desks papers must cross. Besides that, if Clifford and his colleagues are planning some kind of robbery, we would like all the fish to swim into the net at the same time. Precipitate action might cause the break-up of the group, and we'd have to start a trace all over again. The four at the villa have done little so far, and though we've intercepted their calls there is nothing we can yet act upon. Two left this morning and have not yet returned but there are no signs they have fled as such. It's business of some kind, we conclude. Observations continue, phones have been tapped, we have a trace of two mobiles, but we are reaching the conclusion that though nothing specific has yet occurred, it may be time soon that we move in...'

'Amen to that,' Cardinal said solemnly and finished his coffee.

Nine miles away lay the south-west border of German; to the east lay Austria; under the hull of the boat lay the waters of the Bodensee, the lake forty-five miles long, eight hundred and twenty-seven feet deep. Grout had read these details in a guide book at breakfast and now as he sat on the deck of the chartered launch with Cardinal and Enders and raised his face to the morning sun he felt again that he was a world away from his native Yorkshire.

He had never been a travelling man.

He knew the hills and dales of Yorkshire well enough but he had never desired to see the rest of the worlds; it was true he had taken a few packaged flights to European destinations but he still preferred the hills and fells of northern England. Now, as the boat surged slowly across the blue surface of the lake and sharp points on sunshine seemed to leap up from the bows Grout could hear the conversation between Enders and Cardinal seated behind him at the stern. Enders was telling Cardinal about the commercial fishing on the lake, the steel-hulled fishing boats that set out each morning with their nets.

'It is a pity that you are not a fishing enthusiast,' Enders was saying, 'for there is good opportunity for sport here: perch, pike, trout, blaufelchen.'

'My interests tend to lie elsewhere,' Cardinal muttered.

Grout could not imagine where. He had never been able to discover what Cardinal did in his spare time. Perhaps there was no spare time. But he recognised the determination in Cardinal's tone, and perhaps Enders senses it also: idle chatter was not what Cardinal wanted. He had his mind set on one thing only; he was committed to his search for the man he had been hunting for years and Grout guessed that cardinal's palms would be itching now at the thought of being so close to laying his hands on Clifford at last.

'You see that?'

Enders was gesturing towards the tall, three-storied honeycomb structure glistening whitely at the water's edge as they cruised past.

'Follow it along there: now, just there where you can make out that terrace, and the road slicing up the hillside. Up above there is the villa I've been talking about. There is Clifford and his associates.'

Cardinal was already lifting his binoculars. Grout had inspected them earlier, out of curiosity. They were heavy duty, Second World War, marked with the name of its German former owner. Grout wondered how Cardinal had come by them; they were heavy, and inconvenient, but though Cardinal could have used more modern binoculars more easily, he was clearly attached to the equipment with a history. He remained staring at the villa for a short while and then without a word handed the binoculars to Grout. After adjusting the focus slightly Grout saw the villa spring into sharp relief: he could pick out the white-walled house clearly, and the low wall that ran around three sides of the infinity pool. Two men were lounging there in casual shirts and sunglasses.

'Neither of those is Clifford,' Cardinal said.

'You can tell from here?'

'I can tell.'

Enders leaned forward. 'I mentioned earlier that two of the party have left the villa. One of them could be Clifford, but I'm not sure. As soon as they return—'

'We must move in,' Cardinal interrupted sharply. 'I've waited long enough for this chance. As soon as they return we take them.'

'I think you are right,' Enders replied. 'Everything is ready and in place.'

In the event the action was long delayed. The morning wore on, the sun climbed high in the sky and Enders made a pretence of fishing as the boat rocked gently on the lake surface, ruffled only slightly by the light breeze. The open deck was hot, and Grout slipped under cover of the wheelhouse from time to time, worried that the fairness of his skin could cause him suffering that evening if he stayed in the full glare of the sun too long. Enders trailed his desultory, un-baited line. Cardinal stared doggedly at the villa half a mile away, his attention riveted, looking for signs of movement.

In the late afternoon they received their first radio communication. Enders immediately snapped open his mobile phone and made a call. Grout could hear the faint voice of Enders's informant. He had no idea where the man was located but he clearly had a view of the access road to the villa.

'One man has returned.'

'He came alone?' Enders asked.

'One man only in a car.'

Cardinal gnawed at his lip. Enders glanced at him, waited.

'What do the local police want to do?' Cardinal asked.

'They are prepared to act on your instructions. It's unusual, but it seems you have good contacts and in spite of their misgivings they will do as you decide. This will be an extradition matter, though we can use the European warrants. But they have already told me they have the passport identifications but they do not know whether these men have forged their identities...or indeed, have multiple passports. But, when you say we enter, they will do so. It's up to you.'

Grout was surprised to see indecision in Cardinal's eyes: he knew Cardinal desperately wanted Clifford to be in the villa before the raid occurred, but at the moment he could not be sure the big fish was there. So they waited.

The sun began to dip. Shadows grew longer around the lake and the surface of the water took on a deeper, darken blue. There were fewer boats standing out in the lake now and twinkling lights began to appear along the lakeside. Cardinal's lips drew back over his teeth in a feral snarl. 'We can't wait any longer. There are three men in there. Once darkness falls the task becomes more difficult. We'll go in and take them. I just hope one of them will be Clifford.'

They need luck, Grout thought.

Enders immediately made the call as the launch on which they had been waiting nosed back towards the lakeside. They had a rendezvous point and the boat engine roared throatily into life and the bows lifted as the launch surged towards the shoreline. Cardinal's shoulders were hunched; he was uncertain, concerned, and Grout shared his concerns: the net wasn't tight enough.

They could not be sure their quarry awaited them in the villa.

From the terrace below the villa they could see the broad sweep of the lake, fading blackly into the distance but ringed with jewelled lights, coruscating in the darkness. Grout and Cardinal were walking behind the uniformed German police group; officially they could take no part in this action although it sprang from their presence, in effect.

The non-combatant role had an unsettling effect upon Grout and he suspected that Cardinal also found it irksome not to feel directly involved in the action. But there was little they could do; it was all up to the German police presence. Once the arrests had been carried out Cardinal and Grout could come into their own.

Grout watched while the men were deployed up the terrace towards the gate of the villa. Cardinal spoke from just in front of him.

'What do you think, Grout?'

'It looks efficient, sir.'

'Mmm. But unimaginative. What would you do if you were in there with this little pack marching up on you?"

'I'd try the back, obviously.'

'I wouldn't,' Cardinal said curtly.

'The men in there wouldn't know the back is covered.'

'If they've got any sense they'd guess it was, though. I would. So I'd stay well away from the back wall. So what would they do?'

The detective sergeant was silent for a little while.

'The roof,' he said.

'Right.'

'It can't be covered, though,' Grout protested. 'We can't place anyone up there and I shouldn't think there's any way a man could get off that roof, even if he did climb up from inside.'

'No, I don't think it's possible either but we don't know, do we?'

Grout hesitated and glanced towards the policemen moving up the steps of the villa.

'You think I should make a check, sir?'

'I'm not carrying on this conversation for the sake of it, Grout. What are you still doing here?'

Grout left at once, smarting.

He was angry. Cardinal had that effect on him, the grating of two personalities who would never see eye to eye in human terms.   But their brief experience in working together had brought its rewards in terms of success. It made it no easier to accept their basic incompatibility, nevertheless.

Grout's anger cooled as he walked down the hill and around through the narrow street for he recognized also that Cardinal was right. It would be difficult to make the suggestion to the German police; this was their affair. And Cardinal would have to be there when they entered the villa. But the roof ought to be checked; Cardinal could be right.

He was right.

Grout came back up the hill and found himself in a narrow alley that ran alongside the villa. The roof was high above his head and anyone dropping from it would risk a broken leg or worse. On the other hand it was a flat roof, it would allow a man a running jump, and the roof of the dark building on Grout's right, though gabled, was only twelve feet distant at its high point. Grout walked the length of the alley, staring up wards. In a matter of minutes the police would be entering the villa. If there was to be any break out by the men within it would occur very soon now. There was no time to go back, warn the police or Cardinal. He had to act himself.

A convenient pipe took him to the first gable on the roof; from there he was able to scramble across the tiles to a flat area where he commanded a view of the roof of the villa, slightly above him. He crouched down and waited, checking his watch as he did so.

His wait proved short in duration. He heard no whistles and no noise of forcible entry but not three minutes after he had crouched down he saw a brief flash of light in the air, a window or a skylight opening to the villa roof. After a moment he thought he heard a confused thudding sound but could not be sure. There was the chance that it was the noise of a fracas inside the villa, with the police attempting to overpower the men they sought but such theorizing was thrust from Grout's mind the moment he caught sight of the dark, swiftly moving figure on the roof of the villa.

The man carne quickly, light on his feet. He stepped to the edge of the villa roof and stared down into the alleyway. For a moment Grout thought that the fugitive was going to chance the drop; if he had done so

Grout wouldn't have followed him for disaster would be inevitable. The man on the villa roof came to the same conclusion and with a swift glance behind him began to cast along the roof like a hound seeking a scent. He quickly realized there was no way off the roof and Grout flattened himself against the gable as the man stared across towards him. Next moment the fugitive was stepping back, pacing out a run. Grout admired his coolness because it could be only a matter of minutes before the German police inside the villa came up to the roof in pursuit.

As Grout watched, the fugitive was launching himself into space.

He came down like a dark, ungainly bird, thudding hard against the nearest gable, sliding and crashing against tiles, scrambling and grabbing for hand-holds and for a moment Grout thought that he was going to fall back into the alleyway but the man recovered his balance, clung to the gable, and waited a moment to regain his breath.

Grout stood up.

The two men were thirty feet apart, and Grout was still hidden by the gable he had been crouching behind, but if he waited longer the man across from him might shin down a wastepipe to the alley and be lost to him. Grout stepped forward, his feet scraped against the tiles and he came out into the open.

There was no longer a dark figure against the next gable. Grout had not counted on such a swift reaction from the fugitive; he had hoped for the element of surprise. He heard scrambling feet, caught a brief glimpse of a fleeing man making his way across the flat area of the roof and Grout shouted.

He was rewarded with a bullet.

It came with a smack and a thud. It struck the tiles at his feet, across to his left and shattered several of them and Grout stood stock still in astonishment at being shot at. Not only was the man desperate enough to use a gun but he had even equipped himself with a silencer.

A black, unreasoning rage took Grout by the throat. He was not used to being shot at in the course of his duties. There was something altogether too professional about this turn of events and it enraged him. With a grunt he lumbered across the roof, heedless of the danger from the gunman, and gave chase.

He reached the next gable and caution had not entirely deserted him in spite of his anger. He kept away from the edge, made no attempt to expose himself and peered over. He caught sight of a vague, swift movement some forty feet away and ducked back to shelter but there was no bullet. He looked out again and the gunman had disappeared. Grout took a deep breath and surged over the edge, out into the open, dropping ten feet to a flat piece of roof and glaring around him angrily. The gunman had gone. Grout charged across to the gable top and looked wildly around him. Within seconds he guessed at the man's route; the roof of the next building was perhaps fifteen feet away; the darkness of another alleyway between lay below him. Almost without thinking Grout stepped back, took a run and leapt.

He struck his elbows painfully, barked his knuckles and the edge of the roof drove all the breath out of him but he clung, pulled himself up on to the roof and lay there for a moment, panting. As he did so he heard a curious sound, a mingled cracking noise and a muffled shout. He struggled up to his feet and in the dimness of a clouded moon he saw that he was again on a flat roof, extending away into the darkness, seemingly interminably. Half-way across the roof was a patch of newly laid tar, sealing for the flat area of the roof. To the right of it was a skylight. Grout came forward carefully and his pulse was racing as he waited for the bullet that could at any second come whirring out of the darkness. The skylight was broken. Grout knelt at its edge; it was perhaps fifteen feet square and the glass had been shattered. He glanced back to the tar and guessed what had happened. Whether the gunman had intended going into the skylight or not was unimportant; he had skidded while running across the new tar and he had gone through the skylight.

Grout licked his thick lips, considering' He could wait here, hope the others came along, or he could attract their attention. On the other hand the gunman could be hurt...a fall through the glass could have cut him badly, and when he struck the floor below he might have further hurt himself. Grout peered through the skylight but could see nothing.

He put out his hand, felt an iron stanchion within the frame and then with his elbow he smashed away some of the glass. After only a moment's hesitation he sat on the edge of the skylight frame and lowered himself gingerly through the open skylight, bracing himself on the stanchion. Next moment he was dangling in mid air, holding with both hands to the stanchion and the muscles in his shoulders cracked as he hung. He had no idea how far below him the floor might be.' He had no idea what he might strike. He braced himself for the shock and closed his jaw tightly then dropped. To his amazement it was like falling on to a trampoline. He bounced three times, uncontrollably and farcically on his feet then fell forward on to his face. It took him several moments to realize that he was lying on an interior-sprung mattress.

He was unable to enjoy the sensation. There was a quick sliding sound from the darkness to his left and

Grout rolled sideways, falling to the floor. This time his fall was more painful; the drop was all of ten feet and he realized he had been lying on a pile of mattresses.

A bedding factory; he was in a bedding factory and now it was to be a macabre game of hide and seek among piles of mattresses. There was the hum of machinery in the air but above it Grout could hear the clanging sound of metal, a gun hand banging against a metal door. Grout came charging out into the alleyway between two dark piles of mattresses and he could see nothing but he heard the man at the far end of the factory floor move quickly at the sound of Grout's clattering feet. Grout began to run forward towards the doors at the far end where the fugitive was trying to get out but then once again discretion made him step sideways into the cover of the piled mattresses. There was silence ahead of him.

Carefully Grout moved out, still seeking cover. It seemed as though the man ahead of him could not get out; if that was the case, he might turn like a cornered rat. Grout needed cover. Fifteen feet away from him he could make out the dim shape of a square, glass walled container. Through the glass something glowed, whitely, swirling in an artificial dance. Grout moved quickly towards it and he made out three pot bellied vats.

Next moment the container starred crazily as a bullet smacked into it and feathers drifted out of the shattered opening. Washed and dried, in the like tiny ghosts in the dark air but Grout had no time to admire them. He was on his knees, scuttling for the cover of the vats for he was suddenly aware that the flavour of the situation had changed considerably.

The man with the gun was no longer running.

He was unable to get off the floor of the factory and he would have a little time in hand to make his escape before the police got around to this factory.

Provided he could dispose of Grout.

So now he was coming after Grout. And he had a gun. The silencer thudded again and Grout heard a violent clang as the bullet struck the vat. Grout lurched away from its cover and ran between the piled mattresses once more. He felt far from heroic and was now fully recognizing his own foolishness in coming down into the factory after the man with the gun. He heard the steps coming after him, more slowly, more carefully and the realization that this man was a professional, doing his job with care, slowed Grout's own blood.

The man wasn't panicked even though the police would soon be here. It was necessary that Grout also should maintain a cool head. Iron steps loomed up ahead of him. He went up them quietly and carefully. At the top of the steps he found an unlocked door and eased himself through it. Beyond was a low ceilinged room opening up into another, piled high with burlap bags. Grout turned at once, realizing he had walked into a dead end.

He was too late. He heard steps on the rungs outside.

Grout looked quickly around. There was no weapon to hand, just bags, piles of soft bags, full of feathers. He could think or nothing less useful to repel a man with a gun. He looked up above him and caught sight of a chain dangling from the ceiling. He climbed up on one of the piles of bags and reached for the chain. It was looped into a hook, suspended from a trapdoor in the ceiling and Grout realized that the chain was used for lifting bags up through the trapdoor.

For a moment he thought of trying to force open the door, climb through to escape from tie man coming up the stairs but there simply wasn't time. He could hear the man nearing the top of the iron staircase and in a matter of seconds he would be opening the door and there was nothing Grout could do about it.

In desperation Grout unhooked the chain and linked the short hook at its end into the topmost bag of feathers. He clutched it to his chest and stood upright. The chain swung, creaking, the door opened and the man with the gun stood there, arm raised as Grout threw himself from the top of the bags.

The explosion seared across his eyes and he felt as though he had been struck in the chest with a sledgehammer. He was knocked off balance, swinging sideways on but even so he collided violently with the man standing in the doorway and with a surprised shout the man went down. The mouth of the bag was torn open by the fall and it spilled feathers in a cloud, a vast white mass of down. It filled the air, it covered Grout and the man underneath him so that they were forced to spit out the fine down as they fought for breath and for life. Grout was the heavier of the two but they found difficulty in getting to each other. The gunman tried desperately to free his right hand but it was the one thing Grout had seized for immediately and he now hung on the man's wrist twisting the gun away from his body, hammering the man's hand on the floor, trying to make him release the weapon.

A fist took Grout at the side of the head and the white down was suddenly shot with violent coloured stars. The two men rolled away from the bags and collided with the door. The gunman grunted as the edge of the door struck his skull but he gave no sign of weakening and he swung again at Grout's head, a wild swinging blow that lost direction and ended behind

Grout's left ear. Grout felt the fingers of the man's right hand loosen their grip and with one final, grinding blow to the floor he succeeded in forcing the hand open.

The gun clattered to the ground. They rolled again, struggling furiously and the fugitive was underneath Grout but fingers reached for Grout's eyes, gouging furiously so that Grout was forced to jerk his head away. His reaction was enough to give his opponent control of the situation momentarily; he bucked violently and Grout lost his balance. He was thrown backwards against the wall, struck his head and once more crazy colours flashed before his eyes. In a daze he rolled, expecting a fist a boot some form of attack from the other man but there was none. He whirled on the floor, half sitting and saw the other man through a haze of drifting white down, staggering away from Grout, but not towards the door.

He was crouching, bending, searching and Grout knew what he was looking for. The down impeded his vision, slowed him down but not long enough to allow Grout recovery of the situation. Grout struggled to his feet, desperately attempting to regain his balance in one wild charge but already he could see that he was too late. The man was gasping in triumph as he bent down, groping through the drifting down, picking something up from the floor.

The gun.

Grout stood riveted in the centre of the room, unable to move. It was as though it were a bad dream. It all had an element of suspend animation about it; movement seemed slow and agonized when it came, as though Grout were watching a slow-motion replay of a situation. The man came up from his crouching position and he was turning to face Grout. He rose to his full height, turning as he did so and the thunder of the gun was excruciatingly loud in the confined space...the silencer had been damaged, or released when the gun clattered down.

The bullet went nowhere near Grout, it had been fired too quickly, in nervous reaction. But Grout knew that the next unhurried bullet would wing its way home straight into his chest. He saw the man facing him, saw the arm raised to a classic firing position, the professional making the kill and the chain was to Grout's left. Almost instinctively he grabbed it swung it and it described a dark arc through the still drifting down.

The second bullet went into the ceiling. There was a scream from the man, thickening suddenly changing to a gurgling sound and then he was down on his knees clutching his throat, making animal sounds. Grout staggered towards him, saw that the hook on the edge of the chain had entered the man's throat, half lifting him from his feet with its impetus, and had torn into his neck diagonally. From the spurting blood, Grout guessed it had torn the man's jugular vein.

There was nothing Grout could do about it. In a sick daze he fell to his knees and then lay on his back, as the last feathers came down, small fluffs of down. Just before he lost consciousness he was vaguely aware of the tiny snow white down that hung, lifted by a light current of air that was undetectable by him, so light that it could hold only the finest feathers.

Only the very finest feathers.

Eagle's feathers.

CHAPTER TEN

The coloured concentric circles stopped whirling and shimmering and a deep blue darkness descended.

Grout opened his eyes and the darkness turned to a dim, flashlit greyness. He was aware of people and voices and someone saying, 'He is regaining consciousness.'

Grout struggled to sit up and found himself looking into the face of Detective Chief Inspector Cardinal. It was Cardinal's niggled face, when his lean ascetic features seemed more drawn than ever and the thin line of his lips was marked with a downward turn that signified his displeasure.

'You're still alive, then, Grout.'

Perhaps it was this he was displeased about. Grout put one hand to his forehead and groaned. He felt very sorry for himself and then he remembered the other man and the sickness came back to his stomach.

'Clifford?' he asked stupidly.

The displeasure in Cardinal's mouth became more apparent and was matched by his tone of voice. 'It wasn't Clifford. What the hell were you doing down here anyway?'

Grout opened his mouth but it seemed pointless to try to explain: he guessed that Cardinal's question had been largely rhetorical in any case.

'Is he .. . dead?'

'Very. You really opened up his throat with hook' Cardinal was staring at Grout with a vague curiosity. 'I'll be interested to read your report on whole matter.'

Grout struggled to his feet; Cardinal rose also, making no attempt to assist the detective sergeant. He seemed to be in a thoroughly unpleasant mood. 'I thought he might be Clifford,' Grout muttered again.

'Well, it wasn't Clifford. The bastard wasn't at the villa. This man' the guy whose lights you put out, he was called Schneider. So much we've got from the others we caught in the net, but that's all they're saying up to now.' He paused, observing Grout sourly. 'You were damned lucky we found you so quickly, Grout. We heard the last couple of shots and came running, thought you might need assistance.' Cardinal pulled a face. 'You could have tried something less messy in your methods of self defence. And more efficient, too. This chap Schneider will have nothing to tell us now.'

Grout swallowed hard, fighting off the nausea still affected him and ignoring the throbbing of his skull. 'There might be something on him that'll be useful to us, sir.'

'There might be,' Cardinal said coldly, 'but you'll be glad to hear that the German police are looking though his pockets. I shouldn't think you'd want to be doing that. There's blood everywhere.'

Grout was sick in the corner of the room.

They returned to the villa within half an hour. Schneider's pockets had been emptied but there was little there of assistance to them, except his pocket-book. The interrogation of the men arrested at the villa was carried out by the German police and Enders joined them, leaving Cardinal and Grout to look through the contents of the pocket-book. It contained a wad of euros in a thick wallet. Schneider's passport was stuffed into the back of a separate pocket-book, together with a flight ticket to Schiphol Airport. Grout stared at the photograph of the man he had killed and the photograph stared back, dark-haired, beetle-browed, neat collar and tie. It could have been the photograph of an aggressive businessman. Grout said so.

'A professional killer, in fact,' Cardinal said, glancing at the photograph. 'And according to Enders, one of the best contract killers in Europe, or was...Enders tells me that his assignments haven't been too numerous of recent months, maybe he was losing his touch.'

'You mean Enders knows he was a professional killer?'

'Of course.' Cardinal appeared surprised at Grout's innocence. 'But knowing t man was a gun for hire is another thing from actually catching him with one in his hand. That's why he was so keen to put a bullet in you, so keen to get away. This would seem to be one occasion when he was carrying his gun and was cornered. Even so...'

Cardinal was silent for a moment, staring at the airline ticket. 'Even so,' he continued thoughtfully, 'he might have had another reason for getting out so urgently. Maybe he wanted very badly to get to Amsterdam. Now I wonder why he would want to do that?'

'I can't imagine,' Grout said. 'Who are the others in the villa, anyway?'

Cardinal continued to stare, almost absentmindedly, at the airline ticket. 'One of them is English, from Clifford's organization. I guess he's been acting as Clifford's personal aide, and we've got enough on him to put him away for a while in England. I'm letting Enders deal with him, though, to see if he can pick him up on any offences over here. The other two chaps are Germans...I don't know where they fit into the picture at all.'

He broke off, looked up and fixed his gaze on Grout. 'We've been concentrating on other matters. Grout...things have been pretty hectic these last thirty-six hours. We've not had much time to chat. I'd like to hear what you make of it all.'

'All, sir?'

Cardinal waved a negligent hand. 'Yes, you know what I mean. Rigby at Chesters Fort. Eloise Parker at Sheffield. And now this little hideaway on the Bodensee.'

Grout hesitated, eyeing Cardinal carefully. 'You want all my theories, sir? I mean, adding what I learned from Philip Proud?'

Cardinal smiled thinly. 'Oh, yes, that as well. You've kept those cards close to your chest so far. So, unburden yourself now, Grout and tell me all. Give me the advantage of your intellectual curiosity.'

Grout's chin came up at the jibe but in a stubborn, determined tone he said, 'I think the whole thing should start with Philip Proud's evidence, sir.'

'I'm listening, Grout.'

'All right, sir. It all started when Philip Proud wrote a thesis in which he dealt with the Paduan Conspiracy, an attempt on the life of Lodovico Sforza. In that thesis he also mentioned that one of the conspirators escaped with a priceless jewel—'

'All very romantic,' Cardinal said dryly.

Grout ignored the interruption.

'The conspirator reached England. Some of what I now say can't be proved at this stage but it's reasonably intelligent guesswork, sir. The conspirator was murdered by Sforza's assassins but succeeded in hiding the jewel from them. It was passed on to his son, who like him was a stonemason by trade. The trouble was, neither Bollands or his son could do anything with the jewel. If they had attempted to sell it they would have been traced by Sforza's assassins. So they kept it hidden. Bollands died; his son remained equally careful. Then, after the son died, part of the son's

154

headstone was removed at the insistence of the bishop and that's as much as we know...'

'And it was all a long time ago.'

'Yes, sir. But we do know that the stone was inscribed DIBUS VETERIBUS. That's the reason why the bishop ordered it out of Alnwick churchyard. And we do know that Chesters Fort was broken into and a legionary piece, also inscribed DIBUS VETERIBUS was stolen.'

Cardinal smiled thinly, but some of the vagueness had gone from his eyes. 'So go on with your theorizing, Grout,' he said.

'My guess is that the stonemason Bollands forged that legionary piece, used it to hide the jewel, and passed it on to his son. The carving, the wording, it was a clue to the location of the jewel. It's my belief, sir, that Joseph Rigby came by some knowledge of the jewel of the Madonna, or its likely whereabouts. He went to Philip Proud and conned him into letting him read the thesis. From that he got what he wanted. It was Rigby who broke into Chesters...'

'There's a hell of a lot of guesswork in what you say, but at least that fact,' Cardinal said quietly, 'that's something we can prove, now. Before we left England I read the forensic report from Newcastle. There's stone dust and so on among Rigby's clothing that links him with the break-in.'

Grout nodded. 'He was after the legionary piece...which I suspect we will now never find. It would have been broken up to retrieve the jewel.'

'You could be right.'

Grout cleared his throat carefully, eyeing Cardinal. 'It's also my belief that Clifford didn't know about the jewel of the Madonna.' He knew this was something Cardinal would not wish to hear. It would undermine Cardinal's conviction that his old enemy Clifford was behind all nefarious dealings in this matter. Hurriedly, he went on, 'Not then, at least. But I think Clifford did discover that Rigby, who was one of his hired men, was branching out on his own. He didn't like that.'

'He wouldn't,' Cardinal interrupted. 'I know the man. His gang would be under a strict code of conduct; and little ploys like lifting a jewel for your own purposes would be very much against that code. I'm still not convinced by what you're suggesting, but go on.'

'Clifford didn't like Rigby's action so he called off the meeting he'd planned, either came north himself or sent someone, and when Rigby came out of Chesters...'

'Bang'' Cardinal murmured. 'So you think Clifford made off with the jewel?'

'Yes, sir.'

'And what about Eloise Parker?'

Grout shrugged. 'It's not too clear, sir, but I gather she was Rigby's girl friend. He must have told her to meet him at Chollerford so that they could take off together with the jewel and live happily ever after. Gilbert, that photographer chap, he said she seemed to be waiting for someone. But when Rigby didn't turn up...

'She thought about a dalliance with Gilbert, and then probably had second thoughts...Actually,' Cardinal drawled, 'I can help you there, Grout, because forensic also tell me that she was out at Chesters early that morning. Before Paul Gilbert was up and about, wandering in his priapic daze.'

'You mean she met Rigby at Chesters?'

'No. They seem to think she might have gone up to the site shortly after he was killed.'

Grout pulled at his lower lip with a finger and thumb. He nodded, seeing the picture in his mind's eye. 'She came up, found Rigby's car, maybe even found

156

Rigby stretched out on his back with his head bashed in. That would have sobered her up well enough. And then she scarpered, fast. Wise girl.'

'But not wise enough,' Cardinal said. 'She shouldn't have stayed in Sheffield.'

'I agree, sir. It all fits. She went back to the flat, scared as hell, and laid low. But it wasn't difficult to find her. Paul Gilbert managed it, and so did Clifford. And it was Clifford who got to her first. He killed her because she could talk to the police, maybe even talk about the jewel of the Madonna...'

'Assuming that Rigby had told her what he was up to in the first place. He probably gave her some hints, arranged for her to join him at Chesters before they lit out, got themselves out of the country beyond reach of Clifford...' Cardinal sat down and stretched out his legs. 'But that just about brings us up to the present...and we don't know too much about why Clifford came out here to the Bodensee. Chasing after the jewel? Or meeting someone he could make a deal with? Maybe our friend Enders can help us out on that one.'

He was able to, a few hours later. The police were still involved with searching the villa but the men who had been arrested had already been hustled off to Constance. Enders looked tired; he had been mainly responsible for the interrogation.

'We have now identified the two men we captured at the villa. In fact, one is German, the other Swiss. They were remarkably consistent in their stories but Interpol soon gave me the back-up information I required to call their bluff. They are both dealers.'

Cardinal raised his eyebrows. 'Dealers ... and more?'

Enders smiled. 'As you say. They have legitimate businesses in their respective countries, but a great deal of undercover trading is done in addition.'

'You mean they're receivers?' Grout asked.

'I believe the traditional term in England is "fence", and that is why they're here,' Enders said. 'According to them it was an arrangement that had been in place for some time.'

'Clifford was getting rid of some of his stuff to them?'

Enders nodded emphatically. 'These two gentlemen are among a group in contact with Clifford. They act as go-betweens with auction houses and museums. Clifford acquires the items, arranges for transport into Europe, usually to a warehouse in Basel and men like these then take over the items, cover trails by dealing amongst themselves, raise false transactions and documentation to provide plausible provenance and then sell the stuff on to respectable collectors or museums, through auction houses that are prepared to turn a blind eye to the shadiness of the transactions. Museum directors of the most eminent reputation can be surprisingly lax when they see an exciting piece that will enhance their own, legitimate, collections.'

'You have physical proof to back this up?' Cardinal asked.

'There is enough evidence in the house itself to justify our making an arrest and the German authorities are more than willing to co-operate in your investigations. They have already uncovered a considerable amount of property which would seem to have been stolen. As far as we can make out Clifford must have made regular trips across to the Bodensee, which was a useful location for the distribution thereafter throughout Europe and the United States...'

'And once the items were distributed, Clifford would fade from the scene,' Cardinal said grimly, 'with the artefacts under different ownership.'

'As you say. The pity of it all is that we have not got our hands on Clifford himself.'

Grout knew it was a thought that would already be burning at Cardinal. He did not voice it. Instead he said, 'Has any jewellery been found?'

Enders looked vaguely surprised and smoothed a hand over his bald head. 'Not so far. The material these people have been dealing with consists largely of larger pieces looted from various locations in Iran, Europe, Asia and international organisation is involved. Clifford was the UK controller. But these two fellows...the Swiss and the German...they do not handle jewellery. I believe that Clifford would have fenced something like that in London, not here. The market there is a good one, I understand, though you will know more of this than I...'

'It's a good one,' Cardinal growled in assent. 'So these two men deal mainly in stone artefacts, antiques and paintings then?'

'That is so. Notably, of recent years, items looted from Etruscan tombs.' Enders stared at Grout. He was a perceptive man and he was aware of a certain tension in the detective sergeant. 'You have a reason for asking about jewellery?'

Before Grout could answer Cardinal cut in. 'Tell me, Herr Enders. Why was this man Schneider here?'

Enders shook his head and frowned. 'I do not know. He does not fit into the picture. The normal pattern. These men are dealers, criminals of course, but are not really known for what you would describe as strong-arm activity.'

'Unlike Clifford, of course. But he was at the front end of the business. Still, could Schneider have been brought along as a bodyguard?'

'We do not believe so. The dealers have had a long association with Clifford and other activists. They would not have had reason to fear violence.' There was little doubt in Enders's tone. 'However, Schneider, his assignments are of a pattern. He is not a man who is hired to protect. He is a man contracted to kill.'

'But this could have been a rather different assignment from the ordinary,' Cardinal said casually. 'Let's assume that Clifford has in his possession a jewel.'

Enders considered for a moment. 'A jewel of value?' he said slowly.

'Worth the ransom of seven kings,' Grout said in a quiet voice.

Enders glanced sharply at him and then at Cardinal. 'This is so?'

'Let's suppose,' Cardinal said sweetly.

'In that case it is possible,' Enders considered, 'that Clifford would then find it advisable to have a man like Schneider ... But a gunman is still out of place here at the villa. These men, the Swiss, the German, Clifford...they would have worked on a basis of trust, believe it or not, and Schneider would be a dangerous outsider.'

'But he was here,' Grout said.

Enders shrugged in puzzlement.

Cardinal shifted in his chair. 'Of course,' he said, 'Schneider may have been told to wait here for Clifford. Or to join him. Somewhere.' He stroked his chin thoughtfully and his thin lips seemed to reflect a certain inner happiness that surprised Grout. 'If Clifford got his hands on a jewel of such value, where would he go from here to get rid of it?'

Enders stared at Cardinal and weighed his answer carefully. 'If it is a jewel of the value Sergeant Grout describes there is only one man he could go to, and one place. The man is called Le Cochon...The Pig. The place...it would of course be Amsterdam.'

The satisfaction showed in Cardinal's features. He smiled. 'So there we are. Schneider had in his pocket-book a ticket. A first class flight...to Schiphol Airport.'

Cardinal and Grout took a taxi with Enders from Schiphol Airport and came in along Churchill Laan, crossed the Amstel Canal and drove along Ferdinand Bol Straat until they reached the Singel Gracht. Enders paid off the driver.

'It is only a short walk from here.'

The three men crossed the canal and walked along its edge. Three moored houseboats at the far bank were silent; beyond them the cars lined the edge of the canal, perched precariously on the verge between the road and the water, seeming to hover among the trees that lined the road like mechanical animals about to leap into the water. Enders led Cardinal and Grout away from the canal and down a side street whose houses leaned in the upper storeys as though trying to catch glimpses of the traffic along the canal. Enders stopped outside the store window full of tourist trinkets.

'In here.'

He walked through the shop, brushed past a surprised assistant and opened the door leading to a narrow flight of stairs. There was obviously some kind of warning system in operation below because as they reached the head of the stairs the door opened and the man who stood there beamed a welcome. 'Come in, gentlemen. An unexpected visit, Herr Enders, but a pleasant one nevertheless.'

Grout could understand why the man was known as Le Cochon. He was definitely of porcine proportions. The Pig. He was almost six feet tall and built like a massive boar. His eyes were almost buried in deep rolls of fat, his cheeks were covered by a bristly beard, sharply trimmed at the chin and he seemed to roll as he walked. But for such a big man he was surprisingly light on his feet and there was a measured confidence in his tone that suggested he was not a man who feared much; more, he himself would be a man to be feared. If not by the police, at least among his own kind.

He ushered them into the room. It was carefully furnished, but Grout noted that the furniture was of a sturdy kind, necessary, he guessed to support Le Cochon's huge frame. Grout guessed the man would weigh at least twenty stone. He had a beaming, expansive smile, as Enders introduced first Cardinal, then Grout to him.

He waved them to seats, and as they settled into capacious armchairs offered them hospitality. They refused the drinks. He did not seem offended.

'I must crack the whip over my informants,' he smiled, displaying expensively kept teeth. 'Normally I am kept well informed with regard to likely visitors to my domain, but this time...I have no secret sources of information that tell me English policemen are visiting me. I guessed you would be policemen, of course, not just because you are in the company of Herr Enders. It is simply that...shall I say...all policemen have an air, an aura about them. And the English police, they have the brightest aura of all. And the language, it can be so imprecise that I welcome the opportunity to use it. Is that not so, Herr Enders?'

Cardinal and Grout watched as The Pig waddled to a liquor cabinet in the surprisingly luxurious room and poured himself a liberal dose of schnapps.

'You gentlemen have made it clear you will not drink on duty, this I realize but you will permit me ... The room, you like it?'

It was as flamboyant as the man was huge but Grout had little time to enjoy it for Enders came straight to the point. 'I thought I'd find you here rather than at your legitimate place of business.'

The Pig spread deprecating hands. 'You make a jest, of course, Herr Enders. You know well that all my business is legitimate. I own this shop and it is necessary that I visit it from time to time in order to keep an eye on it. After all, managers are notoriously unscrupulous and one can so easily be robbed blind by people one trusts...'

'You come here,' Enders said pleasantly, 'to conduct under the counter deals, sell and buy doubtful merchandise, and meet some of your less respectable friends. I know it, and you are aware I know it. You see,' he added for the benefit of Cardinal and Grout, 'our friend here has a flourishing business in the diamond trade. Unfortunately he cannot resist the occasional illicit deal.'

Le Cochon gave a rumbling laugh that ended in a grunt of pleasure. 'Herr Enders will have his little joke.' The big man was smiling but there was a wariness in his little eyes as he looked at the men facing him. He sipped at his schnapps. His glance turned to Cardinal, calculating.

'I understand it has to be big business before it will interest our friend here,' Cardinal murmured, holding the big man's glance.

'That is so,' Enders replied solemnly.

'I wonder why he waits here today?' Cardinal said as though The Pig was not in earshot.

'Something big,' Enders surmised.

'A jewel, perhaps?' Cardinal suggested, pursing his lips thoughtfully.

The big man spread his hands wide again, smiled, sipped at his schnapps and looked at each of his visitors in turn. They sat in a tight half circle, silent for a little while. Le Cochon was smiling into his drink. At last, he murmured, 'A jewel, you say.'

'A very important one,' Cardinal said softly.

'Very valuable?'

'Worth the rhea ransom of seven kings,' Grout said, on cue.

The Pig sighed, drank his schnapps with a flourish and looked sadly at the three police officers. 'Ah...Such a jewel...I have not heard of something like this coming onto the market. I fear I cannot help you.'

'I understand there is no one else who can help us,' Cardinal replied. 'I am told it has to be you. It is too big for anyone else.'

The Pig glanced sourly in the direction of the Interpol man as though he felt a friendship had been betrayed, and shook his head sadly. 'It has not come to me.'

Cardinal seized on the unspoken words. 'You mean you expect it will be coming to you?'

The Pig looked at Cardinal appreciatively. 'No. I don't think it will be coming to me.' He hesitated for a moment. 'This jewel... you say it was a big one, so?'

Cardinal was silent and the other two followed his lead. The Pig stared moodily at his empty glass and sighed again. 'Such a jewel...Well, I have to admit there has been a whisper... But it is not for me. I will hazard a guess...you are seeking the man Clifford, is not that so?'

Enders jerked his head in a surprised nod and Cardinal leaned forward. 'He has been here?'

'No.' The Pig shook his head in denial. 'But he has been in touch. I tell you this so that you will have confidence in me, Herr Enders, in spite of the slighting remarks you have made in the past. I am an honest man. I desire only to assist the police, as a legitimate man of business. Yes, Clifford he telephoned me three days ago. He told me about ...a jewel. One of great value. He asked if I was interested...'

'And you arranged to meet him.'

The little eyes flickered from the face of Enders to Cardinal. 'We were to meet this afternoon, at five. There were to be ... ah ... discussions.'

'Concerning the jewel?'

'You must understand. It was a negotiation only. I would consider handling the...onward transmission of the item, though I assure you I would have done it only I was made certain that there was nothing illegal about the matter—'

'Come, come,' Enders reproved him. 'You knew Clifford. It would have had to be a doubtful transaction."

The Pig smiled. 'A man has to live, Herr Enders. But I am being frank with you. We were to meet. If all was well, the jewel was to be handed over tomorrow. Negotiations today, transactions tomorrow.'

Cardinal frowned. 'A moment ago you said that it has not come to you, and that you do not think it will be coming to you. But now you tell us arrangements have been made.'

The Pig made no reply but folded his hands over his huge stomach and closed his eyes. In a sharp, exasperated tone Cardinal said, 'Two people have died already and this jewel has been the prize. This is not simply a case of stolen goods, of receiving stolen property. This is a case of murder.'

'I know.' It came out as a grunt. The Pig opened his eyes and they were bright and red, gleaming.

'You know about the murders of Rigby and the girl?' Cardinal said in surprise. The Pig made a negative gesture with his hand, rose with difficulty and lumbered across the room with a slow gait. He stared out to the street and the canal with his back to Cardinal and the others.

'A man called Rigby and a girl...I know nothing of such matters. But I know that murder is involved.'

His voice took on a more thoughtful tone. 'Parking space in Amsterdam is so restricted. During the day, and again in the late evening it is so difficult to find parking spaces. The cars line the canals and so often the careless driver does not properly put on his handbrake or engage gear and his car trundles forward, perhaps slips into the canal. Do you know that Amsterdam has a special service, for recovery of such vehicles?' He paused, spread his fat hands wide. 'A car was pulled out of the Amstel this morning, at dawn, I understand... There was the body of a man discovered in the interior of the vehicle. A report of the incident appeared in the newspaper this afternoon. It was accurate as far as my own informants have been able to assure me.'

'Has the man been identified?' Cardinal asked.

Le Cochon waddled across to the cabinet to pour himself another drink. 'I am told his papers were in order, and recovered. An American tourist, it seems.'

'What has this to do with your meeting regarding the jewel?' Enders asked, irritated by the big man's nonchalant attitude.

The Pig shrugged. 'This accident, it tells me the jewel will not be coming to me.'

Cardinal caught the emphasis on the word accident. He rose to his feet angrily and walked across the room. He stood belligerently behind the gross figure at the

166

window, and in a harsh voice he said, 'I don't understand. What has an American tourist with the jewel?'

The Pig turned. His fleshy face was expressionless. 'The dead man's passport identified him as one Rudolf Kling. But Rudolf Kling was not his real name: it was merely an assumed identity.' He smiled blandly, savouring the moment. 'You will know the man in question as your friend...' His little eyes were fixed on Cardinal. 'Clifford.'

CHAPTER ELEVEN

The Amsterdam police did all they could to help but the information they could offer was little enough. Of the fact that it was a case of murder they had no doubt. The car had been discovered at dawn by a boat proceeding along the Amstel and within minutes the police and the fire engines had arrived. It had taken them an hour to winch the car out of the canal and there had been nothing they could do for the man inside.

'How did he die?' Cardinal asked brusquely.

'Of drowning. But he had been struck on the head. He must have been unconscious when the car entered the water.'

'How do you reconstruct the crime?'

The Amsterdam detective pursed his lips. 'We think that he was struck from behind, at the back of the head. He was carried to the car, placed in the passenger seat. The car was driven along the Amstel to a quiet area, the driver parked it, pushed the unconscious man across the seat, closed the door and pushed the car into the canal. It would have sunk within minutes.'

'Is there no chance of finding a witness?' Cardinal asked.

'The area where the car entered the water is unfrequented at night. During the day it is used by lorries delivering goods...it is a piece of wasteland. No witnesses.'

'Whose was the car?'

'It is a hired car,' the Amsterdam man replied. 'It was hired in the name of this man Kling.'

'Clifford.'

'As you say. His passport states the name Rudolf Kling.'

'It's Clifford all right.' Grout had been with Cardinal when the corpse had been identified by him and he had seen the blank loss in Cardinal's eyes. In a sense Cardinal was feeling defeat; he had wanted to get Clifford, it was an obsession that had driven him for years, and it had almost come to a climax this week.

Now, it was anti-climax and Clifford was dead.

'Did you find anything in the car?' Grout asked suddenly. The Amsterdam man raised an interrogative eyebrow.

'Anything of value,' Grout added.

'Nothing. The car had been little used.'

Cardinal cast a contemptuous glance in Grout's direction as though chiding him for even thinking the man who murdered Clifford would have left the jewel in the car.

'I presume your officers have already checked on his hotel, and searched his room'

'They have.' The Amsterdam man smiled. 'But you are quite welcome to take a look also. We are only too happy to co-operate. Nevertheless, I am sure you will find nothing has been overlooked'

The hotel Clifford had used was an expensive one in the centre of Amsterdam, much frequented by American tourists. Cardinal and Grout made their way through a plush lounge to the reception desk, introduced themselves and asked to be taken to the room used by Kling. The receptionist appeared embarrassed and explained that she should first contact the manager. She vanished in a flurry and Cardinal and Grout waited, eyeing some of the camera-laden Americans who wandered into the lounge. While they waited they heard a burst of applause from beyond large doors at the far end of the room and Cardinal grimaced.

'A meeting or a lecture of some kind. I suppose it'll be in Dutch, so that leaves me out. I presume you do speak Dutch, among your other accomplishments'

169

Grout made no reply and the receptionist returned with a harassed expression, called them forward to the lift and hurried ahead of them, a nervous stringy woman, immaculately dressed but flustered. She was clearly not used to dealing with the police. She pressed the button in the lift and remained silent, head down as they ascended. When the doors opened a man stood waiting for them. He introduced himself as the manager, a small, edgy fellow in a dark grey suit and white shirt: his eyes seemed never to stay still, flicking glances about him as though seeking dusty evidence of cleaning staff incompetence. He gestured towards the end of the corridor, and led the way to the room taken in the name of Rudolf Kling.

He hovered in the doorway until Cardinal brusquely told him they would rather look around alone.

The two men worked through the rooms of the suite quickly and efficiently. Within the hour they faced each other and confessed defeat. There was no jewel in the rooms. Cardinal sat down on the bed with a disgruntled expression, then lay back and closed his eyes.

'I don't understand it, Grout.'

Carefully, Grout slid into a chair and stared at his chief. He made no reply and after a moment Cardinal opened his eyes and stared at the ceiling.

'And yet, though I don't understand it, there's something in all this that we should have seen but have just missed. For the life of me I can't think what. But come on, Grout, you're the chap with flair. You're with me to do the thinking'...I'm the honest plodder, you're the bright self-educated man. So what do you make of it all?'

He rolled over suddenly on to his stomach and glared at Grout. 'You theorized about what happened at Chesters and thereafter and I agreed with it, but somewhere we've gone wrong. Where?'

Grout considered, thinking over the events of the last twenty-four hours. At last, hesitantly, he said, 'Time factor, sir.'

Cardinal glared at him, his thin mouth drooping and then he nodded, abruptly. 'Yes, it's been bothering me too. Not so much the time factor, as the timing of events. Clifford skipped from England and came to the Bodensee and then sat there. Waiting. But what was he waiting for?'

'The fences, sir.'

'But why couldn't he arrange for them to be waiting for him? And then again, he left the Bodensee yesterday, or even earlier, and he came to Amsterdam. Then he waited again, here in this hotel. What the hell for? He contacted The Pig then arranged to see him next day. Why not then, immediately? What was he waiting for?'

'I don't know, sir.'

Cardinal growled deep in his chest as though infuriated that Grout could provide no answers.

'There are two other things that bother me. The first is that damned man Schneider. I can't understand why he hired him...though it would have been more than useful to have him here last night, hey? Clifford wouldn't have snuffed it then, would he?"

'Maybe that was the idea, sir. Protection.'

Cardinal snorted indignantly. 'You heard what Enders said. Schneider was a contract killer not a bloody guard.'

'All right, sir,' Grout replied levelly. 'Protection and assassination.'

Cardinal struggled off the bed and began to pace around the confines of the room, with his hands thrust deep into his pockets. He looked decidedly unhappy. 'You know, Grout, it seems to me we've come off the tracks somewhere. We've got bogged down in irrelevant stuff and I'd like to know where. I'm getting a strong suspicion in my mind...'

'I think it has echoes in mine, sir.'

The two men stared at each other. Slowly, Cardinal said, 'You know, I'm beginning to be of the opinion that Clifford ever got his hands on that damned jewel of yours.'

'I'm beginning to think the same thing, sir.'

Cardinal nodded slowly. 'I think that's why he was waiting. He was waiting for the jewel to be brought to him.'

'Or to arrive, sir.'

'And whether he'd made a deal with the feller who had the jewel or not, his intention was to take it...'

'And then use Schneider to eliminate the carrier,' Grout added.

Cardinal smiled. 'It makes a pleasant change to have us both thinking along the same lines, Grout.'

'Even if we're no nearer to a conclusion than when we started, sir?'

Cardinal's smile was replaced by a scowl. He continued to prowl around the room restlessly. 'You know what we'll have to do, Grout. We'll have to go right back, start right at the very beginning and take logical steps. Work through in progression...it's the plodding that brings results, Grout, not the flashes of intuition. We've got to work at this, look at our theories, discover—'

'The non sequitur...'

'The what?'

Grout smiled at Cardinal's suspicious exclamation. 'Discover where we've taken a wrong step in our process of logical thought. I'm just beginning to wonder whether one of our very early premises was correct.'

'Which one?'

'That Clifford killed Joseph Rigby because he felt Rigby stepped out of line, doing his own thing...'

Cardinal stopped his pacing and looked thoughtfully at Grout. His ascetic features mirrored the doubts that were plaguing his mind. Abruptly, he turned on his heel and marched towards the door. 'Good enough. We'll start with that one. Who else could have killed Rigby. But we won't discuss it here. We'll do it downstairs, over a drink.'

Grout followed Cardinal out of the room. They took the lift down to the ground floor and as they entered the reception lounge they were aware of a large number of men emerging from the open doors at the far end. The meeting was over, and the last stragglers were coming out of the lecture room. Cardinal scowled, guessing that it would make a drink at the bar difficult if not impossible to obtain and he told Grout to head for the bar and claim a stool while he returned the key of Clifford's room to the receptionist.

Grout's expression told Cardinal clearly enough that the sergeant regarded the suggestion merely as a ploy to get him to buy the first drink and Cardinal grinned maliciously. He deliberately lingered on his way to the desk: after all, he thought, it would be a shame for Grout to think his intuition about Cardinal was at fault. Let him buy the first drink.

He dropped the key at the desk hut when he walked back through the lounge he thought that Grout had managed to outmanoeuvre him. The detective sergeant was standing there talking to a big, curly-headed man whose face was vaguely familiar to Cardinal. Disgruntled, Cardinal walked towards the two men but his mood changed when Grout turned, smiling, and Cardinal saw the veiled excitement in his eyes.

Grout's tone was cool, and controlled, nevertheless. 'Marvellous coincidence, chief...I've met an acquaintance from Newcastle! May I introduce you?'

He extended a hand to the smiling, handsome man with the frosted sideburns and the friendly eyes. 'Detective Chief Inspector Cardinal...Professor Donald Godfrey.'

CHAPTER TWELVE

Godfrey uncorked the bottle and poured himself a liberal dose of Scotch, then did the same for Cardinal and Grout. He grinned expansively at the others as he placed the bottle on the table and carried the three drinks across to them. 'This is a damned sight better than fighting for a drink in the bar.'

'And the surroundings are certainly more comfortable,' Grout observed, glancing around a suite of rooms that was obviously one of the more expensive in the hotel.

'Ah, well,' Godfrey said carelessly, 'when I travel abroad I feel I ought to do it in comfort, you know? When I agree to give a talk I take my fee, but I also insist that my accommodation is not of the basic kind. If I'm not giving a talk but travelling under my own resources, well, after all, I have my University salary, my television earnings, my book royalties, and I'm single. There's no reason why I shouldn't spend my money of life's little luxuries. No harm in looking after myself, hey?'

'No harm at all, sir,' Cardinal said deferentially. 'What exactly are you doing in Amsterdam, though?'

Godfrey leaned back in his chair and crossed one leg over the other. He took a long sip at his drink and smiled. 'It's a lecture tour. It was planned about eight months ago, you know, though the itinerary wasn't finally decided until March. I've been to Cologne, and this is the second call in the whistle stop. Tomorrow, I'll have a rest day and then it's on to Norway, then across to the States—'

'They're interested in mediaeval England?'

'Fascinated by it! Believe me, my dear chap, they can't get enough of it.' Godfrey grinned again, mischievously. 'I'm thinking of trying to con them into giving me a television series while I'm over there. Why today, in the audience I had downstairs, they were eighty per cent American tourists. And they lapped up what I had to say!' He laughed, suddenly self-conscious. 'But there I go, blowing my own trumpet. Working in television does that for you...makes you extrovert. But what are you two doing in Amsterdam? You're a long way from home.'

Grout glanced at Cardinal and the flicker in his eyes told him to go ahead. 'We're really still making enquiries into that Rigby killing, up at Chesters Fort,' Grout said.

Professor Godfrey pursed his lips, widened his eyes. 'Really? What, here in Amsterdam?'

'That's so. But we've come up to a sort of dead end.' Grout sipped his drink and watched Godfrey as he leaned forward in interest. 'The man who we'd hoped would help us in our enquiries is dead, you see. Chap called Kling.'

Godfrey pulled a face. 'Not my idea of fun, chasing killers around Europe. Still, everyone to his trade, I suppose. And it gets you out of the house, if you know what I mean.'

Cardinal smiled thinly. 'Yes, we try to catch killers, you try to catch audiences. You're an authority on mediaeval England though aren't you? And aren't you a collector of antiques also?'

'Well, in a small way...' Godfrey murmured in a self-deprecating tone.

'I understood it was in a big way.'

The nonchalant smile on Godfrey's face was suddenly less nonchalant, stiffened at the edges. He shrugged, reluctantly. 'I suppose you could say it's ... a collection of some consequence'

'Built up over the years.' Cardinal nodded solemnly. 'How does one pick up bargains though, you know, of expensive items?'

Godfrey frowned, nodded. 'Oh, one develops a flair for these things, an eye, an instinct for picking up the right article...'

'But that means you must also be good at making the right contacts?' Cardinal asked innocently.

Godfrey hesitated before answering. 'What sort of contacts do you mean?'

Cardinal made no sign of replying and there was a sudden silence in the room. Grout broke it by asking pleasantly, 'Aren't you ever afraid that items you pick up might be stolen property?'

Godfrey licked his lips and injected more life into his grin. 'Oh, not much chance of that if you deal with the right people, and it's pretty much a closed circle really. Of course, you have to make sure that—'

'Didn't I hear you were asked to show your collection on television?' Cardinal interrupted. 'You refused, didn't you? Didn't want the collection shown?'

'Yes, that's so ... Another drink?'

Cardinal glanced at Grout, shook his head and refused, saying they would have to be leaving soon. He nursed his glass while Godfrey went to the mini-bar, and poured himself another whisky and his eyes met Grout's. The message was clear enough. Godfrey came back and sat down. Grout leaned forward. 'I had a word with Philip Proud, you know.'

'Oh, yes.'

'He spoke highly of you, for helping him get his degree.'

'It was the least I could do,' Godfrey said deprecatingly.

Grout smiled but there was no humour in his smile. 'I suppose it was ... in view of the fact that you probably had a hand in the disappearance of the manuscript.'

'Me?' A sudden chill seemed to descend in the room. There was a long silence. Godfrey sat stock still, slowly opened his eyes wide and stared in bewilderment at Grout. Slowly his glance travelled to Cardinal, his expression showing amazement at what Grout had said. 'I beg your pardon? What are you trying to say?'

Cardinal chuckled; Grout had never heard him chuckle before but it emphasized the happy excitement the man suddenly felt. 'Very good, very good, Professor Godfrey, that's quite a performance, but your television tricks won't pay off now. Can't you understand what's happened? We're out of the wood.'

'I fail to see...'

'Seeing you here in Amsterdam, it's sort of put things into a new perspective for us. Let me explain.' Cardinal was grinning all over his lean face and he nodded to Grout. 'The sergeant and I, we've worked hard at this case and we've got so far and met a brick wall, with the death of the man we were hunting...Clifford. But a little while ago we were thinking we need to start again, get back to basics, and seeing you here in Amsterdam, well, it's sort of helped things click into place. We're back on track, you see. Taking a different line: asking the original questions but with our focus moving to different areas. And people. And now, suddenly, we're past it, beyond the blockage, both of us. It's all here in front of us, with your presence in Amsterdam. And we both know, Godfrey, we bloody well know how it must have gone down.'

He settled himself back in obvious satisfaction.

'You see, we've been proceeding on the assumption that it was Clifford who killed Rigby. I'm largely to

178

blame for that. I wanted it to be Clifford. I've been chasing him for years. I wanted to pin the killing on him. Oh, we know he killed the girl in Sheffield all right, but my guess is that was just to find out what Rigby was doing at Chesters. He found out, and then killed her to shut her up. Then he went after what Rigby had been after... the same thing you had been after.' There was a strained silence in the room now as cardinal paused. 'The jewel of the Madonna.'

The professor was keeping his emotions under control. 'I haven't the faintest idea what you're talking about,' Godfrey said with the air of a completely surprised man.

'It won't wash, Professor,' Grout said. 'We've haven't really discussed it but we can now see where we went wrong in the beginning, and once we look back to the start of it both Chief Inspector Cardinal and I come to the same conclusion, independently, even if all the pieces don't yet fit into place.'

'It's still largely guesswork, of course,' Cardinal said generously.

'But it's logical and intelligent guesswork,' Grout said. 'The fact is, on a more wide-ranging view of things, seeing you here, apparently innocently, after our recent experiences, I get the feeling that if we were to check through your collection of antiques I bet we'll find some stuff that's been stolen. That's probably why you were reluctant to have your collection displayed on television. After all, one would expect you'd welcome such exposure. But you turned down the chance. I can guess why...' He watched Godfrey carefully, waiting for a reaction. 'Where did you get it some of your stuff from? Joseph Rigby? Le Cochon? Some of the other dealers we've roped in? We'll soon find out if they have had dealings with you. They'll be keen to talk, to make a deal...We don't know how or when you made your contacts but we'll find out.'

Godfrey remained silent, but his fingers were rigid as they grasped the glass in his hands.

'Your mistake, of course, was to let Rigby know too much. What happened? Did you approach him to break into Chesters Fort?'

'Dear me, gentlemen, this really is—'

'Uncomfortable? Oh come off it, Godfrey.' Cardinal's tone was suddenly harsh. 'You read that thesis of Proud's, you linked its finding with your own research and you guessed that the jewel stolen from Lodovico Sforza had eventually ended up in Chesters Fort.'

'Probably cemented inside that legionary statue,' Grout supplied, 'where it had been hidden by Simon Bollands. You wanted it, you decided to ask Rigby to get it for you, not immediately, but near the time you planned your lecture tour. Because you wanted to take it into Europe, to fence it. It would enhance your collection and it would make you rich.'

Godfrey was shaking his head violently but Grout went on. 'The trouble was Rigby got interested; you probably told him too much. His curiosity was aroused and he went to Proud, read the thesis for himself and got the message it contained. You learned of the visit and knew you'd better cover tracks in case others cottoned on, so you broke into Proud's flat and destroyed the thesis in case Rigby, or others, got hands on it. You didn't want anyone else to see what it contained.'

'We appreciate,' Cardinal said sarcastically, 'that you had to support his degree award thereafter. Otherwise, he might have been forced to rewrite it, or could have pressed for a closer investigation into its destruction.'

Godfrey finished his second drink and licked his lips. 'I think this joke has gone far enough' he said thickly.

'No joke,' Grout said. 'And you were far from laughing when you realized Rigby was after the legionary piece. You followed him out to Chesters Fort that night...or maybe you went together. Whichever way it was, when he came out of the Fort he told you he was keeping the statue, and the jewel. So you killed him.'

Godfrey shuddered and rose to his feet. Grout rose with him.

'This has gone far enough,' Godfrey said. 'You're making a mistake. This man Clifford you mentioned, he killed Rigby...all this other nonsense is fanciful.'

'Clifford didn't kill Rigby,' Cardinal said. 'He couldn't have done it. The time factor was against him. He'd called a meeting; he only cancelled it when he learned Rigby wasn't coming. By that time Rigby was already heading for Chesters.'

'Where you killed him,' Grout murmured.

'Clifford didn't even know about the jewel at that stage. He didn't know why Rigby had died.' Cardinal glanced at Grout as he caught the hint of anger in his voice. 'He went after Eloise Parker to find out what it was all about and she told him about the jewel. So he rewarded her by strangling her and then he left the country. He came after you.'

'If this man Clifford was after me,' Godfrey sneered, 'why didn't he turn up at Cologne?'

'Why should he?' Cardinal spoke reasonably, still pleased with himself. 'After all, you'd used your lecture tour to cover your transportation of the jewel...I imagine you left it in your piece of statuary and lugged that around as an exhibit with your lecture notes. He was quite content to let you take it through customs-he

181

guessed there'd be no need to face you until you came here, to Amsterdam. Where he could dispose of it.'

'To a gentleman called Le Cochon,' Grout added, 'who was quite disposed to help us once he learned Clifford was dead. We were puzzled, you see, as to why Clifford waited in his villa, then came here and again waited. Now we know why. He was waiting for you to arrive. Once you were on your way, he flew to Amsterdam. And that's when you were lucky.'

Godfrey lit a cigarette. If his confidence was draining away he showed no evidence of it. His hand was steady; he was still very much in control of his nerves. 'All right,' he said calmly, 'I'll go along with your little charade. Tell me, just how am I supposed to be lucky at this juncture?'

'It's my guess,' Grout said, 'that Clifford intended meeting you with another man. A man called Schneider. He came ahead to fix a meeting with Le Cochon. Schneider was to come later so they would not openly travel together. But when he met you, Schneider was to be there.'

Godfrey laughed, somewhat raggedly. 'This fellow Schneider...what part was he supposed to play in this -'

'He was to kill you, after you'd handed over the jewel to Clifford.'

The laugh died abruptly, and Godfrey stared at Grout then drew quickly on his cigarette. 'You say I was lucky.'

'That's right. Because we got to the villa before Schneider left.' Grout hesitated, then went on, 'I ... I killed Schneider. The consequence was he just didn't turn up in Amsterdam. Maybe some signal had been arranged, or perhaps Clifford phoned the villa, I don't know, but it seems that he must have realized the net was closing and he still hadn't got that jewel. So he came to you, without Schneider.'

''And?'

Cardinal smiled thinly. 'Time for you to talk to us. You tell us.'

Godfrey stared at him seriously. His broad handsome face expressed a certain disdain as he said, 'I've got nothing to say. You two are the ones addicted to fairy tales. I've nothing to add to this romancing.'

'No matter,' Cardinal shrugged. 'We can make guesses. How do you see things, Grout?'

The detective sergeant kept his eyes fixed on Godfrey. 'I think Clifford took a room in this hotel because he knew Godfrey would be here. I think that at some time last night he either broke into this room and searched it for the jewel or otherwise faced Godfrey and demanded it, threatening him with exposure or perhaps death. Either way, it ended with Godfrey striking him down, from behind, of course.'

'A Professor of History overcoming a professional criminal? Really. . .' Godfrey began to laugh but there was a false note to it.

Quietly, Grout said, 'We've already seen an example of your nerve this evening, Professor. You've faced us with complete calm, most of the time.'

'Because I've nothing to hide.'

'You're a good actor, Professor,' Grout continued. 'You're used to an audience, at University, on television. You're controlled. I don't think you'd have found difficulty in convincing Clifford you were scared, or submissive, or under his control. And when he relaxed, you struck him.'

'This is all a lot of nonsense.'

'The hotel would be quiet enough in the early hours' Cardinal said. 'It wouldn't be difficult for a big man like you to haul an unconscious man down the fire escape. He'd have carried a card identifying his hired car. You could have dumped him in, driven him to the

Amstel, and ... there he was. Out of your way. And with no connection between the two of you, apparently'

Godfrey breathed deeply and stubbed out his cigarette with fierce, controlled jab. 'Or in reality. But that's the point isn't it?' he said. 'That's the crux of the whole matter. There is no real connection between this man Clifford and me. All you've said is nothing more than supposition, wild guesswork.'

'Agreed,' Cardinal said calmly.

Godfrey laughed, some of the confidence leaching back into his tone. He stood up, reaching his full height and his ease of manner seemed to grow also. 'There's also another matter. This isn't England. Even if you could prove I'd done all you say, you have no jurisdiction over me. I can walk out of here at any time, free as a bird.'

'Correction,' Cardinal said. 'You could try. But take the sergeant here. He's a big chap. Maybe he'd stop you. Illegal, yes, but in a good cause. Besides, where could you run? We'd be on to you within minutes. I only have to make one phone call and I'd have the immediate co-operation of Interpol and the Dutch police. We can get them to serve an European warrant. The fact is, Professor Godfrey, you're stymied. You haven't a chance. You've a lot of questions to answer. We'll be looking at your collection. And at your recent movements. And who knows what forensics will turn up in due course, when we dredge Clifford out of his last resting place? The room where he died. The car...'

Godfrey stared at the two police officers. His face was expressionless. 'You still can't get over the basic problem. You said yourself...all this is guesswork, supposition. You can't prove a damn thing.'

Cardinal finished his drink, climbed awkwardly to his feet and looked around the room with a self-satisfied air. 'You know Professor, I'm just a plodding jack, that's all. I'm honest, diligent, and unimaginative. I do a job of work as well as I can: doggedly perhaps, stolidly, but that's how it is. Now Grout here, he's different. I asked him to join my squad because he's supposed to be quick, intelligent, and endowed with what we could call flair. Now he is imaginative I have no doubt that already he's thinking just how he could prove these allegations lo,, r make: checking your collection and establishing a link with Rigby, checking your alibi for the night Rigby died, asking forensic to look at the clothing you wore last night, taking prints from the car in the Amstel, and searching this suite, taking it apart to find the jewel of the Madonna.'

Cardinal beamed from Godfrey to Grout and his lean face was alight with an unconcealed pleasure. 'You see, Grout? I admit it. In front of Professor Godfrey here. There are times when we don't get on but I admit the basic truth. You'll make a good jack, and an efficient one in due course. I have confidence in you. I'm going to make a phone call now so you, Grout ... just keep the professor company and start searching this flat.'

He walked out of the room, taking out his mobile from his pocket.

Godfrey seemed turned to stone. In a hoarse voice Godfrey said, 'You'll never be able to prove all this. You'll never pin it on me.'

Grout smiled.

'We think otherwise. In the meanwhile, just stay here with me, Professor, until the chief inspector has contacted the Dutch police. Then ... well, we'll just have to see, won't we?'

It would be a long haul, Grout knew that. But it was right up Cardinal's street and he'd plod along until he came up with what he wanted and needed to put Godfrey behind bars.

With Grout's assistance. So here goes the plodding bit, Grout thought.

Lightning Source UK Ltd.
Milton Keynes UK
UKOW042020240313

208083UK00001B/7/P